CAUGHT IN THE PARALLEL

ROBIN BRANDE

CAUGHT IN THE PARALLEL
Parallelogram Quartet, Book 2
By Robin Brande

Published by Ryer Publishing
www.ryerpublishing.com
Anniversary Edition © 2026 Robin Brande
www.robinbrande.com
All rights reserved.
Cover art by Peter Jurik/Dreamstime
formatoriginalphotos, Adi Arianto, Likanis_flares, Kikmat Studios,
vetortradition, Rizkreativ, Icons8, DGJ, goodprintsshop, Sketchily,
Sinaelgicon, and Marie Dautel/Canva
Cover design by Ryer Publishing
Ebook ISBN: 978-1-946627-13-1
Paperback ISBN: 978-1-952383-22-9
Hardback ISBN: 978-1-952383-69-4

ALSO BY ROBIN BRANDE

YOUNG ADULT STANDALONES

Evolution, Me & Other Freaks of Nature

Doggirl

Fat Cat

Replay

Young Adult Series

~ Parallelogram Quartet ~

Into the Parallel

Caught in the Parallel

Seize the Parallel

Beyond the Parallel

~ Bradamante Saga ~

Book of Earth

Book of Water

Young Adult Self-Help

What If You're Doing It Right? For Teens

CAUGHT
IN THE
PARALLEL

1

I am sitting on a plane.

A private jet.

Someone has put a glass of fresh pomegranate juice in front of me, but I haven't taken a sip.

I've been asked questions: "Are you comfortable? Do you need anything? Are you still jet-lagged? Does the dog need anything? Would you care for an asparagus soufflé?" and I either nod or shake my head. I've barely said ten words in the past two hours, probably for the same reason I haven't tasted that delicious-looking pomegranate juice: my throat seems to have closed up. I'm afraid if I open my mouth I might scream. Because nothing—and I mean NOTHING—is right about this scene.

There is a dog sleeping at my feet.

Not my dog. Not my feet.

There is a guy sitting across from me, the best-looking guy I've ever known, the guy I've been in love with for thirteen years, since I was four years old.

Not the same guy. Just his face and body, skin and voice and hair.

He calls me Halli. I am not Halli. Halli might be dead. Halli might be lost. Halli has left this body—been catapulted out of it, thanks to my brilliant move, trying to save her life—and now it's just me in here, Audie Masters, a girl with absolutely zero clue what I'm supposed to do now.

Not my body. Not my life. Not even my universe.

Oh, great masters of physics, help me.

2

Here is what I remember:

Me, sitting in a sound-proof room in Professor Whitfield's laboratory. The professor and his lab assistant, Albert, explaining to me that time and the laws of physics are just habits of thinking—that things don't really work the way everyone thinks they do.

Me, testing that theory by casting my thoughts three days into the future—three days and a whole other universe away—watching to see what my parallel self, Halli Markham, was doing at that moment. What she was doing was about to get herself and her dog killed by an avalanche in the Alps.

And then I remember this: me hurtling myself at Halli, across the gap between our universes, across the gap of time, me not really a body anymore, but more like a *force*, pushing Halli out of the way of danger, but pushing her . . . where? Into what?

Because the next thing I knew, it was me inside Halli's body, waking up safe in her home, her dog peacefully sleeping at the foot of her bed.

How? How did we all get there? Me and Halli's body and Red?

And where in this universe or any other is Halli? Did I really save her? Or did I just shove her out into some empty void, and it's just me now, alone, trapped forever inside her body and her universe?

And where, for that matter, is *my* body? Is it just . . . gone?

"You all right?" Jake asks me.

I didn't realize I'd been clutching my stomach. Halli's stomach.

I nod and let my arms relax. Jake has been very nice. No complaints there.

Except for the fact that looking at him and hearing him talk freaks me out almost as much as any of the rest of this.

Because he's Will. The parallel version of Will. His name is Jake Demetrios over here, but he looks exactly like the guy I've always secretly been in love with, sounds exactly like him, and even—I know this sounds weird—smells like him. Not that Dial soap smell I'm used to on Will, but something deeper, at the skin level. Which I guess isn't a surprise since they have the exact same DNA, but you'd think a guy in a different parallel universe might slap on some cologne or use a different shampoo or do something to throw you off his scent.

But no, it's that same smell I like to close my eyes and breathe in whenever Will isn't watching and I can get away with it. It's so real to me sometimes I feel like I could spread it on a cracker and eat it. Or swipe a fingerful of it out of the air and smear it behind my ears.

I'm not saying that's normal, I'm just saying that's how it is. And sitting across from this stranger right now isn't really helping me keep a clear head and gather my wits.

Plus every time I look up, he's staring straight at me, usually with this soft sort of half-smile going on that's just too hot for words—I can guarantee that Will has *never* looked at me that way—and it makes it hard to remember that I have a boyfriend now, his name is Daniel, he actually lives in this universe of Halli's, and at some point I'm going to start thinking about him a *lot*, I promise, it's just that right now I have about a billion other things to worry about before I can even get to that.

Like, what is it—exactly—that went wrong? How did I make this happen? I obviously violated every known law of physics, so were there *unknown* laws I somehow tapped into? And can I tap my way out and undo this whole mess?

And what happens to Halli if I do? If I somehow unravel this whole sequence, does that mean she dies after all? I wouldn't be there to save her, so she and Red get buried in that avalanche?

The plane hits a little patch of turbulence, and Jake's foot bumps into mine. I look up and he's smiling at me again, in that way he really needs to stop.

"You're different than I expected," he tells me.

Oh, *really*? I want to say. Maybe because the girl who regularly inhabits this body is the fearless teenage adventurer and explorer that everyone in this universe seems to have heard of. Maybe if this were her in this situation, having to pretend she's me, she'd be all over it and view it as some sort of exciting new challenge: *Expedition Audie.* Pretend to be that physics nerd who spends most of her time in her bedroom reading about quantum particles and probability waves. Oo— dangerous.

"Hm," is all I answer, then I turn to look out the window. I figure the less I say, the better. Fewer chances to mess up and have people realize they've got the wrong girl.

Because I need these people. I need the information they have. And so if I can just fake my way through everything for a few days, maybe I can get out of this before anyone knows what went wrong.

Jake orders himself another glass of juice. "You need anything?"

Yeah, what I need is about five hours alone, all to myself. Time to think.

It's been nothing but go, go since I woke up in Halli's body this morning. I barely had time to come to grips with the fact that I wasn't me anymore, when Red started barking his head off because a car was coming up the road to Halli's house. Then the car stopped, and the person who got out was exactly the last person I ever expected to see.

And for that full minute and a half or however long it took for him to walk from his car to the door, knock on the door, me answer it, and Jake introduce himself— for that brief little time, I was thinking, *Will found me somehow. He's here to rescue me. That's about the most romantic thing I've ever heard of.*

Fat chance. In the same way Will's disgusting girlfriend Gemma has her own—and vastly superior, I must say—version over here in this universe, Will Stamos-Valadez has his own duplicate edition walking around in his same genetic outfit, claiming to be a totally different person.

I'm not sure I can ever get used to these things.

So I opened the door, and he told me right away who he was, and that he works for Halli's father, and that he was there to pick me up and fly me back to Halli's parents' house for some sort of meeting they arranged with her last week.

A meeting I knew nothing about. Halli hadn't

thought to mention it to me before. And now I was going to have to bluff my way through it. It was exactly like one of those anxiety dreams where you know you have a test starting in five minutes, but it's for a class you never attended.

Plus, just like in any good anxiety dream, I was standing there in my pajamas—Halli's pajamas, actually. Jake seemed a little surprised by that. Apparently I was supposed to be dressed and ready to go.

But he looked at me with those dark brown eyes of Will's, and smiled at me in that way Will never does, and it felt even more like a dream than before.

And then he snapped me out of it.

"You must still be jet-lagged," he said. "We saw you just got home last night."

Information. Here was my first clue about what had happened to me between the avalanche and now.

And I knew how he knew.

It was the tracking. Halli explained it to me before. There's a kind of microchip embedded under her collarbone—she said everyone here has them—and her parents can use that to track her whereabouts, at least until she takes them off her list when she turns eighteen. Thank goodness we're both still seventeen. Thank goodness if I'm wearing her body I can at least get some data out of it.

I made a big show of yawning. "What day is it?"

"Thursday," Jake said.

Thursday? My brain clicked into motion. The last time I saw Halli it was Tuesday in her world. How did I lose two days from her life? Where have I been?

If I could see a printout of that—a detailed report of Halli's whereabouts minute by minute since the avalanche—

It might not solve my physics problem, but at least it would give me somewhere to start. Because right now I had nothing—no memory, no facts, nothing.

"I'll go get changed," I told Jake, and rushed off to Halli's bedroom.

The dog came with me, and lay on Halli's bed while I got dressed and packed. I changed into a pair of Halli's jeans and a long-sleeved T-shirt, then stuffed a few more of each of those into the worn-out duffel I found at the bottom of her closet. A few pairs of underwear, a few pairs of socks, I was done. Halli told me once she always traveled lightly. Might as well live up to the image.

I was about to put on a pair of her sneakers when something else caught my eye: Halli's hiking boots.

My heart nearly leapt out of its ribcage.

Because the last time I saw those boots, Halli had been wearing them when we were together in the Alps.

Which meant she'd made it out alive! She'd made it home.

Then my brain had to squelch the whole thing. Of *course* those boots made it home. They'd been on Halli's feet at the time, and I was currently wearing Halli's feet. The boots had come home with me. That didn't prove anything.

I felt the tip of a wave. It was poised there, just waiting to break over me, to crash me down into despair. All it needed was for me to give in, even just a little bit. To be willing to really feel what this whole thing meant.

But I couldn't do that. It might be a great release in the moment to collapse onto Halli's floor and have myself a big, hysterical cry, but how was that going to help Halli? It wasn't.

What Halli needed was my logical, thinking brain. What she needed was for me to be a robot, to not feel, to just take in all the necessary facts and then arrange them in the right, intelligent sequence so I could understand how to save her. I could be emotional later. This wasn't the time.

So I tugged the boots onto my feet. Onto Halli's feet. And I told her dog we were going, and the two of us met Jake back up at the front. He took Halli's duffel from me.

"Ready?" he asked.

"Sure," I said. Which was just the first of the many lies I knew I'd have to start telling from then on.

3

We are flying over water.

Halli told me her parents live in Seattle. That isn't quite true. They live *near* Seattle, which isn't really the same thing, because what Halli neglected to tell me was that her parents own their own private island.

Of course they do.

When Jake points it out to me from the window, I nod like it's all completely expected. Just like I had to be totally casual about the fact that the car he picked me up in earlier was driving itself for most of the way to the airport. All completely normal.

"You've never been here before, have you?" Jake asks.

I'm not sure how to answer. I'm pretty sure Halli

hasn't seen her parents in person since she was a baby. Halli's grandmother, Ginny Markham, raised her, and Halli told me once that her parents never even tried to contact Halli for sixteen years—not until Ginny died last year.

And since then, as far as Halli was concerned, they'd been contacting her too much. I witnessed a few of the "comm" calls between Halli and her mother—the ones where Halli's mother's head floated holographically in 3-D above Halli's tablet—and Halli was always very abrupt and irritable. I know it had something to do with Halli feeling abandoned by her parents, but I also think she just didn't basically *like* them. At least that was my impression.

It's just one more thing I wish I could question her about, now that I'm about to meet them. And have to pretend to be her.

"I know it's been at least ten years," Jake says. "I've lived on the island that long, and I've never seen you. Trust me," he adds, smiling in that way of his and looking me straight in the eye, "I would have remembered."

"Oh," I say. "Mm-hm." Halli never struck me as much of a blusher, but someone different is at the controls now. I'm sure my cheeks—her cheeks—are a nice warm red. I cover one of them by resting my chin in my hand and gazing back out the window.

From the air the island looks green—almost

completely covered in trees. I can see the tops of a few buildings, and a tan border along most of the edge, which I'm guessing is a beach, but otherwise the place looks completely wooded.

And not with palm trees, either, which is what I thought all islands had. It's forest, like in the mountains around Halli's house back in Colorado. I wonder if her parents had all those pine trees imported.

The island is too small for an airstrip, so the pilot parks the jet on the mainland, and Jake and I finish the journey in Halli's parents' own private ferry.

As we come closer to the shore, I get a clear view of Halli's parents' mansion. Although "mansion" doesn't really do it justice. It's more like one of those enormous estates you see in old British period dramas—the ones where people go to balls and then all fifty guests sleep over and send for their carriages in the morning.

The mansion is made of stone and wood and glass. It's four stories high, with huge windows stretching from the bottom floor all the way up to the top, which must give a great view out across the water. And be ridiculously hard to clean.

There's a man waiting for us on the dock. He's dressed very formally, wearing white gloves and holding a glass of champagne.

"Welcome, Miss Markham," he says, and offers me the glass.

"I . . . no, I can't," I say. "I'm . . . too young." I glance at

Jake, who looks like he might laugh, but the servant or whoever he is just gives me a quick bow, and reaches down for the picnic basket at his feet.

"Muffin?" he asks, holding it open. "Cranberry, raspberry, blueberry, ginger—"

"No, thank you," I say, afraid I might hurt his feelings, but there's no way I can eat anything right now. My stomach feels like it's digesting rocks.

"Thanks, Lyman," Jake says, helping himself to a muffin. "Are they—? Right. There they are."

I follow his gaze.

It's a strange thing to see your parents and know they're not your parents. To have to hold yourself back from running to the mother you might never see again, and throwing yourself into her arms and telling her how sorry you are that you disappeared without saying goodbye. To see some other version of your father and think, "No, that's not right. He's not like that. Go back —you've got it all wrong."

They both look older, and heavier, than my parents. And richer. They're dressed very expensively, and Halli's mother is wearing all kinds of jewelry. Both of them look like they get their hair done. Halli's mom's is all puffy and stiff, and her father's looks like it's dyed.

And the way they're walking is all wrong. Both of their strides have this kind of weird aggression about them—like they're marching somewhere to go tell somebody off. My parents aren't like that. They're pretty easy-going and never in that much of a hurry.

But worse than anything else about them, it's the expression on their faces as they come toward me. They don't look happy. They're not excited. This might be the first time they've ever seen Halli in person since she was an infant, and they don't even look like they care.

"Halli," her mother says, opening her arms just a little. She steps forward, clutches me with these sort of bird claws on the sides of my shoulders, and leans in to press her cheek against mine. But she doesn't really go for it, and instead just gives me this kind of air-cheek thing, all the while still keeping me in her death grip like she's afraid I might twist and get away.

"Halli," her father says, giving me a nod.

"Father," I say back.

This seems to confuse him. Halli's mother, too. Then I remember Halli always called her mother by her first name, Regina—never "Mother."

The problem is, I have no idea what Halli's father's name is. I think I heard it once, but if so, it's completely slipped my mind. The best I can do to cover it up is give him the same kind of nod he gave me—stiff and formal, like we barely know each other.

Which I guess must be true. Even if it were still Halli inside here.

Halli's father turns to Jake now, ignoring me. "How was the noise level?"

"Negligible," Jake tells him.

"Vibration?" he asks.

"Non-existent," Jake says.

Halli's dad asks him some more questions about the plane, and I'd like to hear what they're saying, but meanwhile Halli's mother is talking to me.

"How was your flight?" she asks. "That's our newest plane. Your father's only ridden in it once. We hired DeMenici to design the interior. I hope you found it comfortable."

"Yes, I—"

"Dual-cell," she continues, not waiting for my answer. "It's our latest configuration. Uses only half the water of the previous model. It's been a very difficult process—years in the making." She gives me a tight smile. "But I don't suppose you care about that."

"'Course she doesn't," Halli's father butts in.

I feel the need to stick up for Halli, but I'm not sure what to say. So I just give her mother a noncommittal shrug.

Halli's father says, "I have to get back to work."

He pivots around and heads back to the mansion without another word to his daughter.

Halli's mother flicks her fingers toward the man with the muffins. I forgot he was still there, standing at a respectful distance. He gives Halli's mother a slight bow, then picks up his basket and champagne and hurries to get ahead of Halli's father. I don't understand why until I see the muffin man get back to the mansion just in time to hold open the door for his employer.

"We'll try not to take up too much of your time," Halli's mother says. "We wouldn't have to involve you at all if your grandmother had behaved sensibly."

I don't know if she's referring to Ginny Markham dying, or to something else. But in either case, I know Halli wouldn't have liked her mother saying anything bad about her grandmother. So I just don't respond.

"But," her mother goes on, "things are as they are. We should be able to take care of all of it this weekend. We'll have lawyers here, the board will be here—we can settle matters once and for all. Then you'll never have to worry about any of this again. You can go on with your life, your father and I can go on with ours. How does that sound?"

It might sound fine, if not for the fact that she's standing there clasping her fingers together too tightly and smiling in this very tense way. I don't know if that's just how she normally is, or if something weird is going on.

"So," she says. "Any questions?"

"Um . . . no."

"All right, then. Jake can help you get settled. I have to get back to work now, too."

"Okay," I say. "Bye."

It's all very cold and weird.

"Dinner is at eight," she calls back over her shoulder. "Dress appropriately. You're in civilization now."

I stand there and stare after her. And no matter what I think about the whole thing, I know very clearly in my heart exactly what Halli would do right now.

If it were her inside this body, standing on this dock, she'd turn right around, get back on that ferry, and never see her parents again. She'd never answer another one of her mother's comm calls from now until February when she turned eighteen, and then she'd take her parents off the tracking access list and make sure they could never find her or contact her again.

I know that was already her plan—she told me.

But Halli's tracking is the point. I can't leave here until I get it. So like it or not, I'm stuck.

"Well," Jake says with a laugh, "that went well."

I turn to him and look at him with new eyes. He can joke about these people?

"They were nervous to meet you," he says.

"Didn't look like it," I mutter.

He smiles. "Want to take a walk?"

"Yeah," I say. "I do."

4

———

Red couldn't be happier. There's water to swim in, a strong guy with a good arm to throw him a stick—although whenever I catch sight of Halli's arms I'm pretty sure she could hurl a shotput out there, she's so much more muscular than I am. But I'm happy to let Jake do the dirty work, since Red keeps bringing him back the stick, shaking off all his water onto Jake's legs, then standing there panting, ready for the next throw.

"So," Jake says to me.

"So," I say back.

"What do you think of them?" Jake asks.

He picks up the stick again and throws it for Red. I use that time to try to read his face. I can't tell if he's testing me, or just making conversation, or pumping me for information.

The real question is, can I trust him?

He seems like a nice guy, but that's really all I can say. I don't know him. And if he's lived here for ten years, and works for Halli's father, and has never met Halli before, then it's safe to assume he feels more loyal to Halli's parents than to her—no matter how nice he's being to me.

I decide it's best to be cautious.

"I'm sure they're both very good at what they do," I say, even though I'm not really sure what that is.

Jake gives me a look like he knows I've just avoided his question.

"What do you do here, exactly?" I say.

I mean Halli's parents and the company they run, but Jake thinks I'm asking about him.

"I'm apprenticed to your father," he says.

"Oh. Doing what?"

"As a chemist," he says.

I wasn't expecting that—at *all*. Jake is a chemist? Halli's father is one, too? She never told me that. Of course, she also never told me her parents own their own island, so I'm guessing there are a lot of things she left out.

Jake tosses the stick again. Red plunges in after it.

"I met her once, you know," Jake says.

"Who?"

"Your grandmother."

"You did?" I say. "When?" I probably shouldn't act

this excited, but I always loved it whenever Halli would tell me stories about Ginny. She only told me a few, because they seemed to always make her sad by the end, so I'm ready for anybody else to tell me as many stories about her as they want.

"I was young," Jake says. "Eight."

I do the calculation as we walk down the rocky shore. Will—and therefore Jake—is the same age I am. So that means he met Ginny nine years ago—a year after he said he first came to live here.

"I liked her," Jake says. "A lot. She was tough and angry with your parents—you know how she could be—"

I nod, even though I don't know.

"—but when she saw me hanging around, she told me to bring us a couple of horses, and then she took me riding the rest of the afternoon. It was . . . memorable."

I bet it was. From everything I've heard about Ginny, I know she was a fearless, adventurous woman. She brought up Halli to be the same way. I only wish Ginny could have lived long enough for me to meet her.

Although if she had, Halli wouldn't have been on that cliff a month ago, meditating in such a way that our vibrations exactly matched up. I'd never have found a way to slip past the barriers between our two universes, and end up bodily in this one.

And maybe Halli would still be alive if I hadn't.

Or maybe she would have died because I wasn't there to save her.

If I did, in fact, save her. If I didn't just push her out of this body and take it over, leaving her no place to go.

"Halli?" Jake says. "You all right?"

I've got my hand to my forehead, my eyes closed. I can't keep having these thoughts. They won't help. They just make me feel hopeless.

"I'm fine," I say, forcing myself to act normal and keep walking. "Go on. I want to hear your story."

"She told me about you," Jake says. "I already knew who you were from the histories, but she told me some stories I'd never heard."

"Like what?"

"Like the time she lost you in the jungle, and you sat down and cleared a circle around you so you'd be able to see if any snakes crossed it. She said you never cried, you never called for her, you just waited. When she found you, there was some kind of poisonous snake hanging right above you, but you never saw it. And she never told you."

"Huh."

I want to ask him how old Halli was when Ginny took her into the jungle, but I can't, because I should know that. At least I know she was younger than eight, since that's when Jake first heard the story.

Which is just so amazing to me. How does a little girl have the kinds of experiences Halli had, and not turn out completely different from the girl I am? Halli was always so great and accepting of me and my frailties compared to her, and now I'm just even more grateful for that.

I miss her. I didn't even realize how much. Please let her be alive.

I clear my throat. "What else?" I ask Jake. "What else did Ginny say?"

"Well, she told me about the time you broke your arm—"

I look down at Halli's arms, trying to guess which one.

"—and how you broke your ankle—"

They both feel fine to me now.

"—and that your favorite fruit was strawberry, your favorite color was red, your favorite horse was named Samson, and you hated taking a bath and would only do it once a week, and only if you could wear your dive mask and snorkel."

Jake tips back his head and laughs. I crack a smile. Even though I'm supposed to know all this about myself already.

"By the end of the day," Jake says, "I'm sure your grandmother knew she'd made me fall in love with you. Poor kid—heart lost to the famous girl explorer. I'm sure I wasn't the first."

He laughs at himself, and our eyes meet for just a

moment, and I see something there, and Jake probably knows it.

Because he quickly bends down for the stick and throws it out into the ocean, then stands there staring at the dog splashing in the water instead of looking back at me.

And I have an ache here, a pain, right where there's a fresh wound to my heart. It's like an indentation—like a thumbprint in the middle of a cookie. Or like someone plunging his pointy-tipped flag into the earth at the top of a mountain: Jake Demetrios was here. Mark it.

"I've waited a long time to meet you," he says quietly, still gazing over the water.

"I . . ." And then my voice trails off. Because if Halli were here, I'm sure she'd be just as touched as I am by what he just said. And I'm sure she'd know what to say back. But unfortunately that response isn't programmed into the body I'm wearing, so I just have to stand here frozen and mute.

And then Jake has to make it worse. He turns his head slightly, locks eyes with me again, and gives me that half-smile.

And adds, "I'd have to say you were worth it."

5

The voice comes from behind us. "Good afternoon, Miss Markham. I'm Al—"

I spin around and spurt out the first thing that comes to my mind. "Lydia! Your hair!" Then I slap my hand over my mouth to keep it from saying more.

Because she's not Lydia—of course she's not. My best friend—Will's twin sister—is still safely back at home in my own universe, and this person in front of me is an imposter.

She's Jake's twin sister here—of course she is. That makes sense. I just hadn't expected to see her. But now it's all coming together in my mind.

If Jake has lived here since he was seven, obviously he didn't come alone. He would have come with his family—his mother and sister. His mother must work here somewhere. Which is a happy thought, since back home Will and Lydia's mother Elena has been like a second mom to me. I'd love to see the version of her here.

So I can adjust to seeing this duplicate of Lydia, but still—why did she have to ruin her hair? What kind of nutcase would get rid of that long, luxurious cape of black hair that goes all the way down Lydia's back?

And it's not like it's even a stylish cut. It's this crazy, severe bob that's even shorter than Jake's hair. It looks like a little black helmet.

"As I said," she tries again, "I'm Alexa Demetrios. Your mother has asked me to show you to your room."

Her whole outfit is wrong, too. Lydia likes to wear these stretchy, flowy kind of yoga clothes, but Alexa is dressed like a little corporate soldier, all crisp white shirt and straight black skirt and impractical and probably painfully tight shoes. No wonder she looks so pinched.

"Your mother was concerned about the time," Alexa says, casting a scornful look at her brother. "She thought maybe the two of you got lost."

Jake pretends to ignore her and throws the stick again for Red.

"So, I should probably go," I tell Jake. Even though his words are still reverberating in my ear. I was worth the wait?

No, *Halli* was worth the wait.

But he hasn't met Halli, he's met *me*.

Those stories Ginny told him were about *Halli*. That's the girl he's been waiting for.

And by the way, don't you have a boyfriend?

"See you at dinner," Jake tells me.

"Yeah—s-see you." I can hear myself, and it's a familiar sound. It's me all tongue-tied, trying to talk to Will. It's me trying not to let him see how madly in love with him I am.

Ugh. Audie. Snap out of it.

"Come on, Red," I say, and I can tell the dog doesn't want to leave any more than I do. He's completely mesmerized by Jake and the guy's infinite capacity for throwing the stick.

"Come *on*," I say impatiently, and this time Red obeys. But even as he follows Alexa and me away from the beach, he can't help but look back longingly at Jake.

Yeah, I know. I *get* it.

"It's this way," Alexa tells me.

I'm glad for the distraction.

Now I understand how she sneaked up on us. The woods grow almost all the way onto the beach. Alexa leads Red and me through a narrow break in the trees, up a path to a paved road. Something that looks like a modified golf cart sits there waiting for us.

The cart has no steering wheel. Alexa tells it, "Main house," and it starts up on its own, turns around at the first opportunity, and gently drives us back to the mansion.

It was like that this morning, when Jake drove us away from Halli's house. His car had a steering wheel, and he used it all the way up her dirt road, until we hit the pavement. Then the car took over, driving us at a steady pace all the way to the airport.

There were other cars on the road, all of them going at the same pace, too. No one seemed impatient, no one tried to pass— it was almost like everyone was in their own individual cars on the same train track, and we'd all get there when we got there.

I had to act like it was all perfectly normal to me, of course, even though my eyes were darting from the car's control panel to the street then to the other cars, trying to figure out how the whole thing worked. And all the while Jake just relaxed and leaned back against his door, and tried to make conversation with a girl who wasn't talking.

But now I'm glad I've already had that experience, so I can forget about the mechanics and look around at the scenery instead.

There are more buildings here on the ground than I could see from up in the air. Which makes sense, since the trees grow everywhere—up and over and in between. Whoever designed this whole place obviously either loved nature or loved privacy.

Here and there from some of the buildings, people

come out to wave to me. Some of them call, "Welcome, Miss Halli," some say, "Welcome, Miss Markham," and some just stand there checking me out.

I wave back, because it seems like what Halli would do, but the whole thing feels really weird. I'm not used to being any kind of celebrity. I don't know how Halli ever got used to it.

Alexa hasn't said anything to me this whole ride, so I glance over to see what she's doing. She's engrossed in the tablet on her lap, poking at it, swishing her fingers across the screen, reading it—

And suddenly I realize I am such an idiot.

Because didn't I see Halli's tablet on her desk at home? Not her roll-up one that she took with her to the Alps, but a different one, just sitting there waiting for me to grab it. But instead I left it behind.

Maybe I never would have needed these people at all. I'm sure I could have figured out how to access Halli's tracking information on her own tablet, if I'd only worked at it a little while.

But instead I'm at these people's mercy. Instead I'm going to have to trick someone—probably Jake—into showing me the information.

I'm such a dope.

The cart stops in front of the mansion and Alexa gets out. The muffin man—Lyman, I think Jake called him—is standing in front of the enormous wooden doors. He gives us a little bow, then opens the doors for us. I say thank you. Alexa doesn't.

"This is the Grand Hallway," she says, gesturing to the enormous space we've just walked into. "To the left is the dining area. Right is the kitchen and some of the living quarters of the staff. This is the Grand Staircase. Your room is on the top floor. Follow me."

She's already ascending the stairs, but I'm not ready to follow yet. I'm still taking in the bottom floor.

Artwork everywhere. Paintings and statues, luxurious-looking rugs, pedestals holding delicate vases filled with flowers from the garden.

I don't recognize any of the paintings, but something about them just tells me they're super-expensive. Everything in this room probably cost millions. I doubt Halli's parents are like my mom and me, picking up cheap artwork at garage sales and hanging it in our living room just because we think it's pretty.

"Miss Markham?"

"Coming."

Red and I follow Alexa up the stairs. Which is another artistic wonder. The Grand Staircase is as wide as one you'd see in a courthouse or a government building. And the wooden banister is so thick and wide and smoothly-polished, it looks like you could slide down it all the way from the top floor.

I'll bet Alexa has never done that in her life.

But I'll bet Jake has.

"Bedrooms on the second and third floors," Alexa is saying, "guest quarters on the fourth." She looks back and frowns at the sight of Red dripping onto every step. His nails click against the wood. I'm guessing they don't get too many dogs in here. The whole place looks too pristine.

Once we reach the top floor, Alexa turns right. She leads me halfway down the hall, then opens a heavy door. "Here we are," she says. "I hope you'll find it suitable."

I steal a glance at her to see if she's joking.

Because what human on earth could *not* find this suitable? The room is as big as my entire house. I can picture our kitchen fitting in over there, our living room here, my bedroom and my mom's bedroom over there—

"It has a holomusic template," Alexa tells me, "autoadjusting climate, voice-responding request system, integrated bioreactionary induction system . . ."

And five to ten other features I've never heard of and wouldn't know how to work if I tried. I just stand there and try to pretend it's all normal.

Alexa moves on to less technical matters.

"I see that you brought minimal clothes." She smirks toward the battered, scruffy duffel sitting on top of the perfectly white bedspread on the perfectly enormous bed. Someone must have brought it up here for me.

"Dr. Markham always prefers that we dress for

dinner," Alexa says. "If you feel that what you packed might not be adequate—"

She walks a great distance away, then finally swings open the door to the closet. Which is easily the size of our garage. Inside are enough outfits to see someone through an entire year. Dresses, gowns, pants, shirts, coats, sweaters, shoes, shoes, shoes.

As if hearing that last thought, Alexa turns her gaze down toward Halli's dirty, well-worn hiking boots that I've been wearing this whole time. I try to hide one of them behind me. Suddenly I feel very protective of these boots. I might have to wear them with a dress.

Alexa points to a little couch in the middle of the closet. It's good someone thought to put that in there— people probably pass out all the time just from looking at all the clothes.

But what she's really pointing at is the neatly-stacked pile of extra clothes on the couch, in case the ones hanging up aren't enough.

"I've included a few items you might be comfortable with for your sessions with Ferguson. He'll see you tomorrow at seven."

I have no idea who Ferguson is. And I hope she means seven at night.

"Will there be anything else?" Alexa asks.

"Yes," I say, recovering the power of speech. I point to the tablet she's holding. "Can I get—is there a spare one of those?"

"Of course," Alexa answers. She closes the closet door and speaks into the nearest wall. "Celeste, bring Miss Markham a tablet."

"Yes, Alexa," a girl's voice through the wall answers back.

"Anything else?" Alexa asks me.

"No, I think . . ." I'm still processing what just happened. Is this whole room bugged? If so, they're not being very secretive about it.

"Well, if that's all," Alexa prompts me.

"Yeah," I say. "That's all." I just want her to go. I'm feeling a desperate need to be alone right now and absorb everything that's happened to me in the past several hours. There's only so long you can keep going with something new coming at you every five seconds. I need to sit in the dark and be quiet.

Alexa pauses at the door. And then gives me the sickest, fakest smile I've ever seen.

"Welcome, Miss Markham," she says. "We couldn't be happier you're here."

And with that, the world's worst liar leaves the room.

6

It is twenty minutes after eight. I am wearing a very pretty pale blue dress with little white flowers on it. Halli's feet fit perfectly into an off-white pair of flats. Before dinner I took a shower and washed her hair and combed some sort of conditioning oil through it so it gleamed. Now she looks very scrubbed and fresh and presentable, except for one thing:

I am in very grave danger of throwing up.

Because we are sitting on a ship. Not a literal ship, because that would be ridiculous here in the middle of the Grand Mansion, but as far as my inner ear can tell, the dining room is swaying on an ocean with waves rising as high as the windows—sorry, portholes—and it's daytime rather than night, and the seagulls are cawing, and swooping down and up, and adding to the whole sensation of motion.

And there are orcas and dolphins, of course. Splashing into perfect arcs alongside us, frolicking in the waves. The wooden sides of the ship creak in their weathered way, and Red keeps bolting up to bark at the gulls every minute and a half, and it's all not very relaxing.

I have to close my eyes to eat. Otherwise I'm going to be sick.

I guess I should have understood what this mansion was capable of when I took my shower earlier. I stepped into the shower—an enclosure easily as big as my bedroom at home—and as soon as I shut the door behind me, the lights came on.

Suddenly I was in the midst of a secluded forest, surrounded by moss-covered rocks and waist-high ferns. In front of me was a beautiful waterfall, spilling water over the edge of a cliff and splashing down into a misty pool.

As I felt my way around, I realized the only real things were the rocks that made up the shower walls and floor, and the water pouring off a flat rock high above me. Everything else was a holographic illusion.

So I guess I should have been prepared for this dining room, but somehow I'm not. My eyes can't seem to adjust. Every time I see the water tilting outside the pretend portholes, I instinctively lean sideways in my chair. I want to go back to my room. I want to sit in the dark.

We are a small party, here on our ship. Just Halli's parents, Jake and Alexa, and a man who was introduced as Admiral Binghamton. I don't know if that's his real name or if he's playing a part to go along with the show.

The food looks delicious. I just can't eat a bite.

This dining table could easily fit fifty people. All six of us are crowded at one end. Which adds to the feeling of imbalance whenever the waves toss us backward in that direction.

"The rest of the board will arrive tomorrow," Halli's mother tells me. "Several of the members are anxious to meet you. I hope you'll be accommodating."

I nod. Even that makes me queasy.

"Good. Alexa," she continues, "please see to the schedule and make sure that Miss Halli receives her agenda tomorrow morning."

"Yes, ma'am," Alexa answers. "Of course."

"Is your room sufficient?" Halli's mother asks me.

I nod. It feels better this time. Maybe because my eyes are closed.

"Designed by Quala Ingram," she says. "Each room in the house has a different theme."

Oh, really? Then I'd like to request the dining room that takes place on land, please.

"Will she have time to ride tomorrow?" Jake asks. I

peek open one eye to see him. He's looking at Halli's father.

"I expect Miss Halli always does whatever she likes," her father growls.

"She'll be much too busy," Halli's mother says. "This is not a recreational visit. Tomorrow is a work day."

I can't take it anymore—all this talk swirling around me, people talking at me and to me and about me.

I rise to my feet. "I'm not feeling well," I tell them. "I'm sorry, but . . . I have to go."

Red looks happy to come with me. Those imaginary birds must be frustrating.

I lurch out of the room, like I'm trying to walk uphill on a Tilt-a-Whirl. I probably look like I've lost my mind.

I stand just outside the door, trying to get my bearings. For one thing, all the enormous glass walls of the Grand Hallway remind me that it's night. I've just left bright daylight.

"Are you all right?" Jake asks behind me.

I nod weakly. "Can you help me outside?"

He takes hold of my arm and steadies me toward the door. As soon as it's open, Red races outside. He seems to prefer reality, too.

I bend over at the waist and prop my hands against my knees. I take a few deep breaths.

"Do you ever get—"

"Sea sick?" Jake says. "Not anymore. But when the technology first came out."

"That was awful," I say.

Jake chuckles. "You should see the Arctic blizzard. They almost chose that one instead."

I stand upright and start walking. Fresh air is my friend.

"Why?" I ask. "Who would want to eat with all that going on?"

"They thought you would," Jake says.

"Me?" But then I think I get it. They're trying to relate to Halli. Big adventurer-explorer. Of course she'd love to eat on the high seas. Or enjoy some pasta with her family in the middle of a blinding snowstorm. And since that was the scene outside the last time I saw Halli alive, I'm more than grateful they didn't pick that one.

"Please," I say to Jake, "if you could maybe slip them the hint . . ."

"No more?" Jake asks.

"No more."

Red is in the water again. Even though it must be freezing. I can see his head bobbing in the dark.

And for some reason, maybe because I'm too tired, maybe because I'm just tired of pretending anymore for one day, I drop any pretense and just ask my question:

"What am I supposed to be doing here? What's all this about the board and lawyers, and 'We can finally settle this once and for all'?"

If that means I've blown my cover, so be it.

Jake doesn't answer at first. And for a moment I panic and think "so be it" is a really stupid strategy.

But then he comes through for me.

"How much did your grandmother tell you?"

I decide to be honest. "Absolutely nothing."

"Nothing?" He sounds surprised. And probably Ginny did tell Halli all sorts of things, but I wasn't privy to those conversations. These ears may have heard them, but I wasn't wearing them at the time.

I make up a lie on the spot, and hope it at least sounds plausible.

"We never really talked about my parents. Ginny didn't seem to want to, and I didn't want to press her. But now that she's gone . . . there's just a lot going on that I don't understand."

"So she never told you about the company," Jake says. "Or her arrangement with your parents."

"Nothing," I say.

Jakes gives off a low whistle. "So how much do you want to know?"

"All of it. If you don't mind."

"Here." He removes his dinner jacket and drapes it across my shoulders. "This is going to take a while."

7

I'm grateful for the coat.

The air here is cold, and moist in a way I'm not used to. I've always lived in the desert, and up until the past few weeks with Halli, have never spent much time anywhere else. And now just because of her I've already been to Colorado, Germany, the Alps, and now a private island off the coast of Washington. Not to mention a whole separate, parallel universe, if you want to count that.

"I don't know all the details," Jake is saying, "but I've heard a few things over the years, so I'll tell you what I can. Some of it is in the histories, but a lot of it is just gossip among the staff. I hope you don't mind."

"No," I say. "Gossip is fine." In fact, gossip is great. At this point I'm so hungry for information I don't care if it has to come from the friend of a friend of a gardener.

"Your grandmother lent your parents money," Jake says. "Do you know about that?"

"No," I say. "Go on."

"It was back in the beginning—before your parents even knew they would start a company. They had an idea for a water process, and needed some money to test out their theories."

"*Their* theories?" I say. "Both my mother's and my father's?"

"His in chemistry, hers in hydroengineering."

Now I get it. I was too overwhelmed by all the shoes in that warehouse of a closet to really pay attention to what Alexa said before. When she told me Dr. Markham expected everyone to dress for dinner, somehow I thought she meant Halli's father. But now I remember his last name is Bellows. Which means it's Halli's mother who is Dr. Markham.

So both her parents are scientists. And Halli grew up to be an adventurer. Whereas both my parents are social working do-gooders, and yet I became a scientist. Go figure.

"The three of them," Jake continues, "your parents and your grandmother, were in India together at the time. They were visiting different villages so your parents could assess the need. Your grandmother agreed to guide them, since she knew the country."

That makes sense. Halli said even before she was born, Ginny was already a world-traveler, and had spent time in India, among other places.

"Then your parents came up with the idea," Jake says. "The osmotic power system. And right around the same time, your mother became pregnant with you."

A wet chill goes through me, and it's not just from the nighttime breeze. I'm starting to get a bad feeling. I think I know where this is going, but I don't really want to hear it.

"Red!" He's jumped out of the water, and decided the best place to shake himself dry is right behind Jake and me. The back of my dress is soaked.

"Go on," I tell Jake, pausing to wring out my dress.

He hesitates. He doesn't know that I've already guessed.

"I don't know this part for sure," he says. "It could just be people talking."

"They made a deal," I say. "Me for the money."

"Not that mercenary," he says, "but yes . . . in a way."

"So what exactly was the agreement?" I ask. "They hand me over and Ginny finances their company?"

"I don't know if you really want to hear this," Jake says.

"Tell me."

We're heading up a dirt pathway now, leading us away from the water toward the forest behind the mansion. I can't see my way very well, but Jake obviously knows the path.

"Your parents . . ." I can hear him snap a twig off a low-hanging branch. More snaps as he breaks it into pieces. He's stalling, and I know it.

"Jake, you can tell me," I say. "I'd rather know. I doubt it'll change how I feel about them."

"They're not bad people," he answers. "But they're not . . . parental. They don't like kids—they never have, as far as I can tell. I've grown up in this house, and they never liked me or Alexa or any of the other children until we were at least teenagers. They still look right through some of the younger ones like they're pieces of furniture."

"Yeah," I say, "they sound like great people."

He stops on the dark path and turns to me. "I don't want you to have the wrong impression. They didn't give you to Ginny—"

"No, they sold me."

"No," Jake says, "they were honest. They didn't give you to her just because of the money. They knew you'd never have the kind of life with them that you could have with your grandmother. She *wanted* you. Your parents—they just didn't. What they wanted was their work. And Ginny could help them with that. At least that's what I heard."

We start walking again. And I'm not sure how I feel.

I want to be disgusted, but that feels like a fake reaction —like I *should* feel that way.

What would Halli think, hearing this story? I guess there are two sides to it: One, Ginny really did love her and want her, from the very start, and she made a smart decision by offering to take Halli when it was clear her parents didn't want her.

But on the other hand, who wants to hear that your parents just turned you over? That it was an easy trade, yeah, you take my kid, and would you write me a nice, fat check in exchange?

And on the other-other hand, I look at this place, and at the people who own it, and think there's no way in a million years Halli could have been as happy here, with them, as she was with her grandmother. And she'd still be happy if Ginny hadn't died. So isn't it better that Halli had sixteen great years with a grandmother who adored her, rather than sixteen miserable years with parents who didn't care about her at all?

"There's more," Jake says.

"Oh, boy," I say, letting out a breath. "Okay, tell me."

He snaps off another twig.

This time I grab his fist before he can do the whole stalling routine again. "Just tell me."

"Halli, you're freezing." Jake takes my hand between both of his. "Why didn't you say so? We can go back inside."

"No," I say. "I'm fine." Although now that the truth is

out, my teeth feel free to chatter. "Finish what you were going to say. I want to know."

"At least put this on." He helps me slip my arms into the jacket. Up until now I've just had it draped around my shoulders. He folds the front of it across me, then opens up the collar so it warms my neck.

"Better?" he asks quietly. He's still holding onto the collar. He's so close I can feel the warmth of his body, the feeling of his breath against my cheek.

I'm having a hard time finding my voice. I force myself to nod. And even that feels like it takes an incredible amount of strength.

But I have to say something. I know I do.

I can barely croak it out. "What were you going to tell me?"

"I forgot," Jake says.

He doesn't smell like Will, he smells like himself. I close my eyes and breathe it in. I don't know why I ever thought it was the same. This is much, much better.

Then he whispers my name—

—her name—

"Halli . . ."

And finds my lips in the dark.

8

Some physicists say that if you'd just look at the world from a sub-sub-nuclear perspective, the boundaries between objects disappear. Stars become mountains, leaves meld into rocks, and one person becomes indistinguishable from another. We're all just waves in a vast cosmic sea.

I always thought that was just another nice theory, like so many of the amazing ideas floating around out there from so many brilliant minds. But I can tell now from experience that it's not theory. It's an actual, physical fact.

Because when Jake's lips touch mine, and they aren't mine, but another girl's entirely, the molecules of her body dissolve away to the atomic and then the subatomic and then the smallest elemental particles underneath it, until what I feel is the wave of Will and Jake crashing into the wave that is me, and Halli's body is no barrier at all. I feel everything—absolutely everything—just like this body was the one assigned to me at birth, and these have always been my lips, my hands, my mouth—

"What's going on?"

A light burns in our faces.

Jake shields his eyes.

"What are you doing?" Alexa repeats.

"What's it look like, Lex? Get out of here."

I'm too stunned to do anything but back away out of the light.

But it follows me and keeps on shining right in my face.

"Miss Markham, your mother sent me for you."

"Oh . . . okay . . ."

I sort of fluster around for a moment, not really sure what to do, while meanwhile Jake stands his ground.

"We'll come in a minute," he tells his sister. "Get out of here."

"I'm not leaving," she says. "Dr. Markham sent me."

"We'll come in a *minute.*"

"No, that's okay," I tell Jake. "I have to go. Come on, Red. Red!"

The dog crashes out of the brush, and since he's already in motion it feels natural to just run along with him. The path is too dark to go fast, but there's no way I'm asking Alexa for her light.

I can hear her and Jake still arguing behind me, but all I want is the cold air off the ocean and the feeling of movement in these feet. That girl is horrid. This place is horrid. I just want to get away.

There's enough light from the windows of the mansion to guide me the rest of the way back. I'm just about at the doors when one of them swings open and Lyman gives me a bow.

"Are you all right, Miss Markham?"

"Yes," I tell him breathlessly. "Thank you. Thank you for the door."

"Of course, Miss." He bows again.

I squeeze his wrist. "You're really nice. Thank you."

Then I tear up the Grand Staircase before I can run into anyone else. Red's toenails scrape on the wood. Good. I hope he leaves marks. I only wish he were still dripping wet.

Once we get to the top I stop running. I walk past the closed doors, hoping I remember which one is mine.

As soon as I open it, the lights come on, and yes, it's the right room, with Halli's duffel still resting on the bed.

I turn around to lock the door, but there is no lock.

I hate this place.

I need to get my information and leave.

9

Why did I do that?

I keep replaying it over and over in my head.

Okay, and in my body.

Halli's body.

Which is the point.

A guy tells you in no uncertain terms that he's had a thing for you since he was a kid, and you know very well he hasn't had a thing for *you,* and yet you lead him on and let him kiss you—

When the *real* you has a *boyfriend,* Audie, and he's a nice guy and he'd be so hurt by this—

And yes, it was GREAT. It was FANTASTIC. I'm not denying that, and I'm trying very hard not to jump up and down on this soft, springy bed because of it, because really, it was AMAZING, I can't believe how incredible it was to be kissed by him and held by him—

But do you have no morals? Do you have no judgment? Do you have no sense?

It's wrong. It was a trick and it's wrong. It's one thing to pretend to be Halli because I have no other choice at the moment, and I'm hoping I can pretend my way into gaining valuable information that can help me undo this, but it's another thing entirely to carry on some romance in this body with a guy who's completely without a clue about what's going on.

It would be different if I told him the truth. "Hey, Jake, guess what? Oh, man, you're going to laugh at this . . ."

Then say it really fast and hope he doesn't notice: "I'm an intruder from another universe and I've taken over Halli Markham's body, but I'm hoping it's only temporary, glad to meet you, my real name is Audie— so, do you still want to make out?"

Ugh. Never. Wrong.

I need to get out of this place. I can't believe everything that's happened in one mere day—from waking up in Halli's body this morning to kissing some guy with her lips tonight—but what that tells me is I can't afford to spend another full day here and let the whole situation get worse.

First thing in the morning, I have to use whatever charm Jake thinks I have and talk him into getting me Halli's tracking information. Then I need to sneak out of here, figure out a way to get back to Halli's house, and then sit down and concentrate on the physics of getting her back. Without the distractions and the complications of this place.

Of course, it's going to be pretty hard to sneak away when these people can track my every move.

Which is, no doubt, how Alexa found us tonight. Both culprits with our tracking dots going *Beep, beep, beep, here we are, secluded in the woods, obviously up to no good, so hey—come and find us.*

And no lock on the door? Isn't there such a thing as privacy in this place?

I guess not, when even the walls of the guest room are bugged.

I'm so caught up in the misery of the moment, it takes me a minute to process something.

When Alexa was showing me to my room earlier, didn't she ask someone through the wall to bring me a tablet?

And didn't some girl answer back that she would?

I sit up and look around the room. And there it is, sitting on the fancy desk, so small and thin I didn't notice it when I first came in.

I race over to it, and my heart keeps up the sprint.

Because maybe I won't need Jake or anyone else at all. Maybe I can figure out how to access Halli's information myself.

And maybe I can track down Daniel while I'm at it.

And make up for what I shouldn't have done.

10

———————————

"Miss Halli?"

It's morning, and there's a stranger standing by my bed. A girl who looks about twelve years old, holding a tray that looks much too heavy for her. On top of it are a teapot, a coffee pot, cups, various drink accessories, fruit, muffins, and a daisy in a little vase.

The girl smiles as soon as I pry open an eye.

"Good morning, Miss Halli!" She's way too cheerful, too early.

"What time is it?" I mumble.

"Five-thirty. Ferguson said to give you plenty of time to eat and walk your dog before he sees you."

"Who's Ferguson?" I groan. "Why is he torturing me?"

"It's his job," the girl answers.

She presses a button on the edge of my bed, and the curtains in my room scroll open.

"It's dark out," I say.

"I know, Miss. I'm sorry. One moment."

She presses another button, and now the sun is shining, the birds are chirping, and it looks like I'm in the middle of a meadow. A deer grazes in front of my bed. A rabbit hops past. I've barely gotten three hours of sleep.

I bury my face in my pillow. "Please turn it off."

The chirping goes away. So does the sunshine and the meadow.

"I've made you some tea," the girl says. "Just the way you like it, I hope. I also brought you coffee. I wasn't sure which you'd prefer."

What I'd prefer is that the girl go away, but clearly that's not happening. So I wrestle myself up into a sitting position, and the girl quickly sets down her tray and rushes over to fluff up the pillows behind me. It's all a bit too much.

But she seems sweet, and I shouldn't be such a grump. Especially since Halli, unlike me, is probably a morning person.

"What's your name?" I ask.

"Celeste, Miss."

"The Celeste—" I gesture to where I heard her voice yesterday. "—from the wall?"

"The wall, Miss?

"You don't have to keep calling me Miss."

"Oh, I do," she says, nervously glancing at the wall behind the bed. "It's either 'Miss Markham' or 'Miss Halli.' Or, well, I hope you don't mind . . ."

It takes me a second to realize she's afraid calling me just "Miss" is too informal.

"It's fine," I say. "Call me whatever you want."

"Thank you, Miss. Here you are." She hands me the cup of tea, then anxiously watches while I take my first sip.

It's like drinking a memory.

The first time I tasted this spicy, cinnamony tea was on a mountaintop in Colorado. I had just traveled there from my bedroom at home, across the membranes of two parallel universes, and arrived in Halli's universe—this one—wearing just my sleep shirt and boxers.

And even though I couldn't explain myself yet, even though Halli had no reason to trust me—except for the fact that I looked just like her, but what did that mean, really? I could have been an alien clone, sent to eat her brain and take over her body—ugh, not funny, obviously, considering my present circumstances—but Halli brought me back to her camp anyway and made sure I had proper clothing. Then she built a fire and made me a mug of this tea, to make sure I'd be warm.

And now where is Halli? Is she someplace safe and warm? Is someone taking care of her?

I tried to contact her last night. It was after I'd already spent hours struggling to turn on that stupid tablet, and never figured it out.

So I abandoned trying to access the tracking information that would tell me where Halli's body spent those two missing days after the avalanche, and instead decided to use my mind to try to find out where she is *now*.

So I sat here in the dark for hours, mentally sending out signals to her, trying my best to clear my own mind so I could hear her if she were trying to find me, but hours later, still nothing.

Which might mean I wasn't doing it right. Or it might mean she's someplace where the two of us can't reach each other any more.

Or it might mean she's dead. I understand that's a possibility, intellectually, but there's no way I'm ready to believe it. I feel like I would *know* it, here in this heart of hers. And until I really feel it, I'm not going to believe she's gone.

"Miss?" the girl says. "How . . . is it?" She nervously plays with the end of her long black braid. I force myself to smile at her.

"The tea's delicious, Celeste. Thank you. It's perfect."

The girl beams.

And then I have a brilliant thought.

"Can you do me a favor?" I ask.

"Of course!"

I pick up the tablet from where I left it beside the bed.

"I'm kind of embarrassed," I tell Celeste. "My regular one is an older model, and I can't figure out how to turn this one on."

"Oh! Here." She presses the left corner, sweeps her thumb diagonally across the screen, then presses the left corner again.

Instantly, lights start swirling above the tablet. They form into the same company logo I saw on the private jet that brought me out here, and in various places all over the house: OPS. This time the full name appears below it: Osmotic Power Systems.

"Can you show me one more thing?" I ask.

"Of course, Miss."

"I just need to access my—"

Then I stop. I motion for Celeste to lean toward me, and whisper, "Do you think anyone is listening right now?"

Celeste nods. She mouths, "Alexa." Then she says in her regular voice, "So if you need anything else, Miss, just speak into any of the walls here, and I'll bring it to you right away—food, towels, linens, anything you like."

I whisper again, directly into Celeste's ear. "The whole room? What if I want some privacy?"

Celeste points first to the closet, then to the bathroom.

"Are there cameras in here, too?" I ask. "Is anyone watching?"

This time she shakes her head no.

I go back to speaking normally. "Thank you so much for all of this, Celeste. The food looks great."

Then I get out of bed, pick up the tablet, and motion for Celeste to follow me into the closet.

Once we're inside, I close the door. Then I hear a whine on the other side, and open it again to let Red join us. He jumps up on the little couch, on top of the stack of clothes.

"I need some information," I tell Celeste as soon as we're settled down again. I'm still whispering—I can't help it. "I need to look at my tracking information from the last few days. Can you show me how to do that on this tablet?"

"It should be the same as on yours . . ." She takes the tablet from me, and her fingers fly over the screen, pressing and swiping and poking. I want so badly to ask her to slow down, to show me step by step, but that would be giving too much away. Obviously she expects Halli to know how to do this.

Hovering above the tablet now is a new logo: GTS. Global Tracking System.

Celeste hands me back the tablet. "Go ahead," she says, turning her head to the side. "I won't look."

"Go ahead and what?" I ask.

"Enter your code, Miss."

Of course it's password protected. Halli told me it's private information. That's why everyone has to specifically pick the people who are entitled to know where they are.

"I don't . . . remember my code," I say.

"You don't?" I can see Celeste thinks that's a strange answer.

"I never look up my information," I hurry to tell her. "I probably haven't checked it in years." I try to make my voice sound light, even though inside I'm a nervous wreck. This *has* to work. Please let it work.

"Do you think you used Red?" she asks.

"Yes! Try that."

"And what numbers?" Celeste asks.

Great. Letters *and* numbers.

"My . . . birthday?" I guess, even though everyone knows that's a totally crackable password. Especially in Halli's case, when she's famous enough that anyone could know her birthdate.

Celeste enters the code. "No," she says. "Sorry. Want to try again?"

"No, that's okay." Hopeless. This whole thing is hopeless.

So it's back to my Plan A.

"Do you know where Jake might be right now?"

Celeste's face lights up. "He's probably meeting with Dr. Bellows—they have breakfast together every morning."

Dr. Bellows. Halli's father. There's no way I'm going to try to interrupt that meeting.

"Could you . . . I mean, is it possible to get him a message?" I ask. "Afterward?"

Now Celeste looks even happier. "Of course, Miss! What do you want me to say?"

"Just . . . if he could find me, that would be great."

"I'll tell him," she says. "As soon as I can."

"Thanks. That would really help."

"I should probably go," she says. "Alexa will wonder where I am."

She gets up, and is about to open the closet door, when she bites her lip and turns back.

"So . . . if you don't mind me asking, Miss—what did you think of my brother? He's nice, isn't he?"

"Who's your brother?"

"Jake," she answers, like I already knew.

That tea must not have had enough caffeine. Or my ears aren't processing correctly.

"Jake doesn't have a little sister," I say. "Just a twin sister."

"No," Celeste says, "he has me, too."

"But . . . how?" Will and Lydia's dad died when they were little—before I even met them. And their mom never remarried.

But maybe she did here in this universe, and had another child.

"Who's your father?" I ask.

"Oscar Nuñez. He's—

We hear a sound in the outer room. A voice.

"I have to go," Celeste says, yanking open the door. Now we can both hear the voice more clearly.

"Celeste?" it calls. "Are you there?"

"Coming," the girl answers.

"Where were you?" the voice asks. It's Alexa's.

"Sorry," Celeste says. "I was . . . I had to—"

"She was showing me something about the shower," I lie to the wall. "We were in the bathroom. We didn't hear you."

A slight pause, then Alexa's voice again. "Very good, Miss Markham. Sorry to bother you. Is there anything else we can bring you this morning?"

"No, thank you," I say. "Celeste has done an excellent job."

Celeste smiles at me. I like the girl. Much, much more than her sister.

"Celeste, return to the kitchen," Alexa orders. "I need to speak with you."

"I'm coming," the girl answers.

I motion for her to come toward the closet again. Then I whisper in her ear. "Will you get in trouble?"

Celeste shakes her head.

"Thanks for all your help," I say. "I really, really appreciate it."

"I'm so glad you finally came here," Celeste says. "I've been waiting my whole life."

11

It's ten minutes to seven, and I'm dressed like a doll. A workout doll, to be exact.

I'm wearing one of the outfits Alexa said I should wear for my session with Ferguson: matching navy blue workout pants and sporty workout jacket, with a red workout shirt underneath. Even the navy blue shoes with the fancy red laces look like they go with the set. I feel like I've just been taken out of the box and handed all my accessories.

I have absolutely zero interest in exercising this morning—which is what I'm guessing is in store for me, based on the outfit—but I can't see how to get out of it. Until I can talk to Jake and somehow get him to give me the tracking information, I'm stuck doing whatever people would expect Halli to be doing.

I descend the Grand Staircase, hoping I might run into Jake after all and not have to waste any more time, but instead I find Halli's mother.

She's just coming out the dining room, and when she sees me, she pauses and looks me over, then gives me a slight nod. Apparently I'm dressed appropriately.

"Off to see Ferguson?"

"I guess," I mutter.

"Waste of time," she says, "when we have so much more to do." She raises her palm before I can say anything. "But I know—we had an agreement."

That's interesting. I wish so much Halli had told me about the whole arrangement she had with her parents about coming here. I have to keep finding out about it in dribs and drabs.

"Does that dog have to go everywhere with you?" Halli's mother asks.

"I'm . . . sorry, but yes." I don't feel like explaining that he doesn't like being left alone, and besides, the truth is I'm the one who needs him. He's my only left-over connection to Halli's life.

"Well, you'll have to leave him in your room during the board meeting," she says. "I'm afraid we're a little more formal here than you're used to."

"I can't . . . do that," I say.

"Halli, be serious. This isn't one of your campouts in the woods. This is a professional, corporate board meeting. Some of our members are flying in from

Europe. I assure you they're not used to seeing a *dog* at one of our meetings. We have very high standards here."

And yep, if Halli hadn't already left yesterday, I'm pretty sure she would have left right now.

I need to get away myself. I may not be able to leave the island just yet, but I can at least escape this conversation.

"I should probably get going," I say. "That Ferguson guy must be waiting."

"Halli, he works for *us*," her mother says. "He can wait all day, as far as I'm concerned."

I glance over at Lyman, the doorman, and catch his eye. He quickly looks away.

Halli's mother flicks her hand at me. "Fine. Go. But remember, the rest of the day is for meetings."

What meetings?

"Alexa will bring you your schedule. Then don't forget—the board meeting is at four. I'll have Alexa escort you."

"No, that's okay, I'm sure I can—"

"I don't want you to be late," Halli's mother says. "Unlike Ferguson, the board should never be kept waiting."

Then she clicks off in her heels to some other part of the building, leaving just me and Red and Lyman.

I close my eyes for a moment and take a deep breath. I'm feeling shaky. That mother of Halli's is exhausting. Plus this whole place is getting to me—why does every single thing have to be so hard? I'm tempted to head upstairs again and hide out in Halli's closet for the rest of the day.

But Lyman is already holding the door open for me.

"Good morning, Miss."

"Thank you, Lyman. Can you tell me where I'm supposed to go?"

He directs me down the path to a white building I can see in the distance.

"Have a good morning, Miss," he says.

I give him a weak smile and head on out the door.

It's only a short walk, but I take it slowly. Red bounds on ahead, happy to be outside, but I'm in no great hurry. Especially since the building I'm going to is marked "Gymnasium."

No good can come from this.

12

"Halli Markham!" shouts a voice from inside as soon as I open the door. A man strides toward me so fast it's like he's on wheels.

"There we are now, Miss. That's it. Ferguson Haney. Fine to meet yeh." Instead of shaking my hand, he squeezes my bicep. "Aye, now that's how a lass should be."

"Uh, hello, sir."

"Not 'sir,' Miss—never sir! Your folks'll have my hide. It's Ferguson to you, Miss, nothing else."

"Okay," I say, "sorry."

"No harm, no harm."

His accent is Scottish, I think, and he looks a little like a bulldog: short, powerfully-built, with his gray hair squared off into a crew cut. If only he had an underbite, it would totally complete the look.

He sweeps his arm across the empty gym, a room as big as our auditorium at school. "Barely used, I don't have to tell you. Don't know why they keep me on—grateful for the work, don't mistake me. But your folks aren't much for the strenuous life. Mental, yes—don't fault 'em there. But physical, no."

Red finds a comfortable spot on one of the padded benches beneath a window. Meanwhile Ferguson continues his rant.

"Told me, 'Outfit it the way you want, Ferguson. Nothing but the best.' Then the most they can spare me is twenty minutes a day—twenty minutes, lass. You think they even sweat?"

I'm about to guess no—

" 'Course I make 'em sweat," he says. "I know my job. Burn off all that alcohol they're always drinking. Then they're right back at it, that and the rich food, one step forward, five steps back, and they wonder why they're getting old. How old do you think I am?"

"I have . . . no idea—"

"Fifty-nine next month," he says proudly. "How old was your granny?"

"Uh . . ." I quickly try to remember. Did Halli ever tell me? Then I remember she's the same age as my Grandma Marion, minus a year for dying. "Sixty-four?"

"She were a fine lady, that Miss Virginia," Ferguson

says. "Had my eye on her that time she came. Too busy setting your folks right—had a temper, that one, not saying she weren't right—but I woulda loved to court her, don't mind you knowing. Classy lady, that one."

"Thank you." I don't know what else to say.

"Disciplined," he says. "Fearless. Like you, Miss Halli. Don't know how your ma turned out so different. 'Course, knew your dad's folk, not a decent one among 'em."

"Wow, okay . . ." I look nervously around at the walls.

"They can't hear us in here, lass. Insisted on it. Told 'em, 'You want my undivided attention, I get yours. No messages, no emergencies, no outside intrusions.' Just twenty minutes a day—you'd think I cut 'em off from civilization. Race outta here to see what's happened. Twenty minutes and maybe the world stopped spinning, better check."

I have to laugh at that.

"But you have time for me, don't you, Miss?"

"Sure," I say. "I guess." I mean, what else would I be doing right now—sleeping?

Ferguson slaps his hands together. "That's fine, then. Two hours every morning, another hour in the afternoon, if you can spare it."

"Three hours?" I say in horror.

"Please, Miss," he says. "Make an old man happy. Been planning it ever since I heard you were coming. A whole week's worth, get your fingerprints on every piece of equipment. Shake the rust off. Let 'em do what they're here for. Finally get your folks' money's worth."

"I don't know . . ." I say. What I really mean is, "You're out of your mind."

Ferguson slaps me on the back. "Welcome to it, Miss Halli! Ah, you're a fine-looking lass. Knew it from the pictures, but always better to see someone in the flesh. You don't disappoint—I'm guessing that lad Jake thinks the same thing."

"He . . . what now?"

"Had to arm wrestle him to see who'd go for you with the plane. Let him win, poor lad. I was young once. C'mon, now, let's get you started."

He jogs over to the corner of the gym, and waits for me beside a rope. It's about as wide as my wrist, and hanging from the ceiling. From the ceiling two stories up.

"Something easy, loosen you up. Want gloves, or you like it bare-handed?"

I stare at the rope, all the way up to the top, and can't believe this is my life. I can, however, believe it was Halli's.

She would have loved this—every bit of it. She would have bundled this guy up and taken him home. She would have loved the playground of this gym, with all the different ways to test out her strength.

But I'm not equipped for this life. I don't know what

I'm doing. I might have the appropriate muscles and stamina that come with Halli's body, but I don't have any of her coordination or talent. I don't know how to physically do the things she can do. It would be like someone giving me a superhero outfit and expecting me to know how to fly.

And it's not only the physical, it's the mental: it's the fact that it's my brain inside here, not hers, and I only know however much I know. I thought it would be easier to fake my way through this and try to figure things out. But it all keeps coming at me all the time—the technology, the family history I know nothing about, the relationships I'm supposed to understand, and now some sort of "meetings" all day that I'm going to have to bluff my way through—and even though I know I'm smart, I'm not *this* smart. No one is. It's too much.

And suddenly, I know I can't do it—any of this. I can't keep pretending to be Halli. I might have gotten away with it so far, but pretty soon I'm going to make a mistake, and then someone's going to realize something is wrong.

And then what?

No, really—and then what? What am I going to say? How am I supposed to explain myself? Who besides Daniel would ever believe me? The only reason he was willing to even entertain the idea that I was a visitor from another universe is that I accidentally disappeared right in front of him. So either he was losing his mind or there was something odd about me. He preferred to believe the odd.

But I'm not disappearing anymore—believe me, I wish I could. Go away for an hour, for even five minutes, and take a break from a body and a universe that aren't mine.

And meanwhile, there's another universe out there that's missing the body that *is* mine. What does my mother think? Does she think I'm dead? Did Professor Whitfield explain to her what happened? Does he even *know* what happened? If only I could contact *him*, even instead of Daniel, then maybe the professor and I could figure out the physics of this together. But I'm as cut off from him as I am from anyone in my old life.

What are they all thinking back there? Does anyone believe I'm still alive? Are they looking for me anywhere? Even if they are, how in the cosmos will they find me?

"Miss Halli?"

I turn to Ferguson, and I'm about to make an excuse —I don't feel well, my arm hurts—something. But instead I feel my eyes welling up with tears. I turn away and clear my throat.

"Miss Halli," he says gently, "look at me."

I turn back to him, and feel my mouth start to quiver. Any second and I'm going to lose it.

He takes my hand between his two rough ones and

pats it. "I'll be honest with you, lass. I said you don't disappoint? That's not exactly true. It's not your fault," he hurries to say, "but I noticed. When I saw you come in off the boat yesterday, I thought, 'That's not my girl. Something's changed.'"

Here it comes, Audie, be ready. He's caught you—

"Shoulders slumped," he continues, "head low—I said to myself, 'That's not our Halli Markham. Where's her spunk? Where's her fire? Something's wrong.'"

All I can do is nod. And brace myself for the inevitable.

He pats my hand again. "We'll get you back, lass, don't you worry."

I meet his eyes. "What?"

"I know what it is," he says. "I've lost somebody, too. Knocks the feet right from under you. You think you'll never be the same. You think it's hopeless. But it never is. The sun comes up, you start again. The sun goes down, you rest. You'll get through it, Halli lass, you're a strong girl."

"But what if it's really bad?" I ask him in a choked voice. "What if it's really, really bad?"

"The sun comes up, you start again. It's the only way I know."

13

Two hours. Two hours of brutality, insanity, treating me like a pack mule rather than a teenage girl. Making me haul a sled piled high with weight—including the hundred-pound Red lying on top of the load. Making me run with a pack on my back that's so heavy, for all I know Ferguson himself is secretly hanging on. And climbing up that ridiculous rope, hand over hand, my legs frogging out so I can grip with my feet. Then climbing back down it, slowly, until my fingers feel permanently curled into claws.

I'm not saying Halli's body isn't up to it—it's up to all of that and more. And I'm not saying I don't like it, because in a miraculous, strange way, I do.

Because there's something about that kind of hard physical labor that makes your brain relax for a while.

All you can think about is lifting, moving, running, climbing, and whether you're going to survive to the next physical test.

Plus I'll admit it makes me feel a little better about myself. Maybe I'm a failure at things like figuring out how to turn on a tablet or guessing Halli's password, but row an imitation rowboat as hard and as fast as I can just because Ferguson tells me to? At least I can be a success at that.

"There now, Miss, that should do it," Ferguson finally says. "Save some for this afternoon."

"Are you serious?" I ask, wiping the sweat out of my eyes. "You really want me to come back?"

"I'd keep you here all day," he says, "if there weren't others clamoring for your time."

I pause a moment and catch my breath. "Okay, then," I say. "I'll be back."

I call for Halli's dog, and the two of us head for the door. My perfect workout clothes are so soaked someone might wonder whether Ferguson had me swim laps in them.

Ferguson walks with us to the door.

"Thanks," I tell him. "For the workout."

"No thanks necessary," he says. "Finally feel like I'm useful."

He glances past me, toward the walkway between the mansion and the gym.

"Word of advice, Miss," he says.

"Yes?"

I turn to see what's gotten his attention. It's Alexa, walking purposefully toward us down the path. She's carrying her tablet and dressed like a young executive again, and generally looks like she's ready to step in and run Halli's parents' company if they ever decide they want out.

Since the last time I saw her she was shining a light into my eyes and breaking up a makeout session with her brother, she is truly the last person I want to talk to.

"Don't let her intimidate you," Ferguson tells me. "I know her game. Lexa's a good lass, not saying otherwise, but she likes to lord herself over people when she has no right. She's no better than you, Miss Halli—far from it. She should know her place, and you should know yours."

"Oh," I say. "Okay." But I'm sure I don't look convinced.

"She might not like you being here," Ferguson says. "What I heard."

"Yeah, I think I noticed."

"Bit jealous, I expect," he says. "Bosses' real daughter comes home—where's her place all a sudden? But she'll have to sort that out herself. Not your concern. You hold your ground, understand?"

"Yeah . . . okay."

"Miss Markham," Alexa says when she reaches us. "Ferguson."

He brings his hand to his head, like he's touching an imaginary cap. "Miss Lexa. I'll leave you to it now. Miss Halli, I'll see you this afternoon."

"No, you won't," Alexa corrects him. "Miss Markham will be occupied the rest of the day."

Ferguson touches his imaginary cap again. "As your schedule permits, Miss Halli." Then he disappears back into the gym.

When I really, really wish he had stayed.

"Some of the board members will be arriving this morning," Alexa says. "Your mother has arranged a brunch for them, and would like you to attend."

"Oh, no, I don't think—"

"After that there's a luncheon with the later-arriving members," Alexa continues. "Then a brief interview with a history reporter, then the board meeting at four." She glances distastefully at Red. "Your mother has also asked me to make arrangements for the dog."

"No, that's okay—"

"Dr. Markham insists," Alexa answers, as if that's the final word.

All that power and self-confidence I just felt in the gym is rapidly evaporating away.

"There's also the matter of your clothes," Alexa says. "Your mother has asked me to choose appropriate outfits. We can return to your room right now, if it's convenient."

It's not convenient. None of this is. What I want is

to take a shower, then go find Jake. I want to get my information and leave. I want out of here.

Plus, I can just imagine what that brunch and lunch and interview would be like: a group of strangers firing questions at me about a life I should know off the top of my head. "Miss Markham, what was the Amazon like? How was Mount Everest? Have you ever been chased by lions? Weren't you once surrounded by sharks?"

And what would I do, just stand there and grin? A lot of those people know a heck of a lot more about Halli's life than I do, thanks to the histories Daniel and Sarah told me about. I've only seen a few minutes of the holographic film highlights, but from what I understand, people in this world have been following Halli's adventures since she was a child. If I try to make anything up, I'm going to immediately be exposed. There's no way I can put myself in that position.

"Really, Alexa, please tell my mother I don't feel up to any socializing today. I'm still pretty jet-lagged. I think I should just concentrate on the board meeting."

"I'm sure she'd be surprised by that," Alexa says, "since you apparently had enough energy for a two-hour workout just now."

We both stare at each other for a second. Alexa looks triumphant.

"That's why I'm extra-tired," I say, yawning for emphasis. "I think I need a long shower, then probably a nap. I probably won't wake up until the afternoon."

"I'm afraid your mother insists," Alexa says, smiling.

"Really, I'm not feeling up to it today—"

"Miss Markham," she answers darkly. "This isn't a choice."

And somehow that does it. Something clicks. And every part of me says NO.

What did Ferguson say about me when I first got off the ferry yesterday?

"That's not our Halli Markham. Where's her spunk? Where's her fire?"

And what has he been barking at me for the past two hours?

"Stand up straight! Shoulders back! Gut in! Why're you hunching like a monkey?"

Finally I get it: I haven't been wearing Halli's body properly. And it's been affecting how I behave. How I think about myself. How I've been letting these people treat me.

It's like that polar bear I read about at this one zoo. Always pacing back and forth from one end of his enclosure to the other: five steps up, five steps back, monotonously, every single day.

Then the zoo finally moved him to a bigger enclosure, but as soon as they put him in there: five steps up, five steps back, just like he'd never left. He spent the whole rest of his life that way, in a cage within a cage, never noticing that things had changed.

I'm no different. I've been locked here inside of

Halli's body for more than a day, and this whole time I've been slouching in it, slumping in it, acting like it's still weak little me inside here, instead of burly, fearless Halli.

I owe it to Halli to do better. To recognize that even though I never wanted this, I'm the one in charge of her body now. And however long that might last, it's up to me to live up to Halli's image—to fill out her body to the edges, to act the way she would act in this situation.

So for the first time since I woke up like this yesterday morning, I stand up tall to Halli's full height. I imagine the insides of me pushing outward, stretching to fill in her hands, her arms, her torso, her legs—every last muscular inch of her body.

And even though my mind is my own, I even imagine taking hers on. Thinking the way she might think. Behaving the way I know she would.

And she wouldn't for one second put up with this bullying behavior from Alexa.

"No," I tell her in a firm voice. "I'm not doing any of that. I have other plans today. I agreed to come here for the board meeting, and that's all. You can tell my mother I'll see her there. Until then, leave me alone."

And then, without waiting for her permission, I brush past Alexa and stride toward the mansion. After a few steps I start running, because that's what Halli's body wants to do right now. I stretch out her legs and pump her arms, and her dog runs along with me, and as soon as we reach the doors, Lyman opens them for us and smiles at me and I smile back. Then Red and I sprint up four flights of stairs because we want to, and we can, and because Halli surely would have done that.

Then as soon as I'm in my bedroom, I collapse.

Not because I'm tired, but because I'm happy.

I've never told off anyone in my life, and it feels so good I can barely stand it.

I can do this.

Halli would do this.

And today, no matter how hard it is or how many times I fail, I'm going to keep trying, Halli, and I'm going to find you. I'm going to figure this out and save you. We're going to fix this.

That I promise you.

Someone has obviously been in my room.

When I roll over after a few minutes of gleeful mental replay of that whole scene with Alexa, I find there's an outfit laid out on my bed: a pair of Halli's jeans, a red checkered shirt, and a pair of Western boots.

Alexa has been here. This must be her idea of an "appropriate outfit" for the brunch Halli's mother scheduled. Maybe the dining room has been switched over from its sailor theme, and now it's been reset to "cowboy."

I can't deal with it at the moment. I shove the clothes aside. What I want most right now is a nice long shower to wash away all the sweat, and to give me some private time for thinking.

But it's hard to just let your mind wander when you step into the shower and it turns into a jungle. The waterfall yesterday was in a peaceful, quiet forest, but now there's a party going on with tropical birds screeching to each other and imaginary monkeys swinging down off the vines. One even splashes into the pool at my feet, and I have to step back to make sure I don't crush him.

How do people live like this? Wouldn't they prefer boring old moldy tile and a gunked-up shower head like I have at home? At least you can think in a shower like that.

I get out as soon as I can, dry off, and wrap myself up in Halli's robe that I brought from home. There's a much fancier one hanging from a hook in the bathroom, but I'd rather stick as close to Halli as I can right now.

It's not like any of the clothes I packed in her duffel are mine, but at least they feel closer to being me than all the ones hanging in that fancy closet. There was a strange comfort to putting on her pajamas last night, and even if Alexa hadn't already laid out Halli's jeans, I probably would have worn those today anyway. I'll just pair them with one of Halli's shirts. These people can't turn me into someone I'm not.

Which is hilarious, since I'm someone I'm not anyway.

I come out of the bathroom, ready to get dressed and go find Jake, but I see I'm not alone.

"How was your exercise, Miss?"

It's Celeste, and she's just setting out all the food she brought up on another tray. A huge bowl of oatmeal, more tea, coffee if I prefer that, strawberries, more muffins, sliced bananas and kiwi and melon, a freshly-baked loaf of bread, three kinds of jam, two different kinds of juice—

"Celeste, who made all this? Don't they know I'm only one person?"

She smiles. "It's my mother. She's head cook." Celeste lowers her voice to a whisper. "I think she's showing off."

I slice off a hunk of bread and smear it with raspberry jam. "Well, you can tell her I'm impressed." Then I realize I can tell her myself—if she's one of the people listening. "I'm impressed! Mrs. . . ."

"Demetrios," Celeste says.

"Oh, right. Demetrios!" I call to the walls.

Celeste giggles. "Only Alexa can hear you. But I'll tell my mother what you said. You'll make her very happy."

"Did you find your brother for me?"

"He's waiting for you," she says with obvious delight. "He said he'd like to take you riding. He told me to bring you down to the stables as soon as you're finished eating."

Now I'm beginning to understand the outfit.

"Did you lay out my clothes for me?"

"Yes, Miss. I hope that's all right.

"It's fine. You made a nice choice." I mentally take back all the mean things I was thinking about the clothes.

Although the truth is I'd prefer wearing Halli's hiking boots today—they fit my mood better than some fancy pair of cowboy boots. But I don't want to hurt Celeste's feelings.

I pick up the tray and carry it toward the closet. I'm getting used to spending an unnatural amount of time in there. Once Celeste and Red and I are inside, I tell Celeste the problem.

"Alexa's going to know, since you just said it out there—and they'd be able to follow my tracking, anyway—but I don't think anyone's going to be happy with me going riding right now. I'm supposed to be at some brunch, then a lunch after that—"

Maybe it's because of my workout, or maybe it's because I just realized I'll be missing both those meals, but I'm suddenly totally starving. I wolf down half of a muffin.

"Oh my gosh, this is amazing!"

"I know," Celeste says. "My mother is the best cook in the world."

"I need to meet her," I say. "Please—can we arrange that today?"

"Yes! She'd love it. You can meet my father, too. Except—what are we going to do about the riding?"

"I'm just going to have to go for it," I say. In part because I'm feeling all Halli-ish right now, and in part because seeing Jake and talking him into giving me Halli's tracking information is far more important than whatever Halli's mother wants me to do. I just have to stand firm.

"You like my brother, don't you?" Celeste asks. "He likes you."

The delicious muffin sticks in my throat. "Um . . ."

"I know I shouldn't say that," Celeste hurries to add. "But . . . he talks about you all the time. He's shown me all your histories—we've watched them over and over again—ever since I was little."

I can feel my face growing hot. Even though it's not even me Celeste is talking about.

And I have to remind myself that no matter what my fluttery little heart is saying right now, the only thing I want from Jake is some data. That's it. Focus.

"Your brother is really great," I say. "It's just . . . it's kind of complicated. I can't really explain it, but . . . yeah, so, I don't know."

"Oh." She looks disappointed. "I'm sorry—I shouldn't have asked. Please don't tell Jake I said anything."

I reach over and squeeze her knee. "Celeste, I think it's sweet how much you like your brother, and all the nice things you say about him. If I had a little sister, I'd want her to be just like you."

"Really?" She seems so relieved.

"Absolutely," I say. "Now how are we going to sneak me out of this mansion?"

15

Celeste and I make a plan to meet out on the path in about ten minutes. I know my whereabouts won't be secret for long, but at least Lyman can tell people I left alone. I don't want Celeste to get into trouble.

I change into the cowgirl outfit, and when I dig my hand into the pocket of Halli's jeans, I find a loose hair tie in there. Perfect.

I pull Halli's long brown hair back into a ponytail, the way she was wearing it when I first met her. I thought it looked like a horse's tail then—thick and shiny and long. It seems appropriate for the event I'm about to try to lie my way out of.

Because there's no doubt the real Halli Markham is an accomplished horsewoman. I've seen footage of her riding a pony in Mongolia when she was only three or four years old. Jake said she had a favorite horse named Samson. I'm sure she's been riding all over the world, on who knows how many different horses.

I am not that girl.

The best I can do is balance on my bicycle. I don't climb up on enormous mammals that might throw me or kick me or run away with me. Just a policy I have, and I think it's a good one.

I meet Celeste on the path Jake and I took through the woods last night. The memory of running back on it through the dark is still a little too fresh. As is the event that led to that retreat.

I'm pretty sure Jake must be thinking about that, too.

I need to come up with a good strategy. Not only for avoiding horseback riding, but also for dealing with Jake.

It's hard to say which of those situations feels more dangerous right now.

"The stables are up and over here," Celeste says, pointing, "then down the hill a little. Not very far."

As we walk along, she points out some of the other buildings. "That's the pool house, and that's the conference building, and those are more guest quarters . . ."

And once again, people wander out of buildings to gawk at me. They pretend they have something to do outside—check the sky for clouds, snip off a flower bud, scrape something off a shoe—but it's pretty clear they're just curious about Halli. It's weird, but I guess I get it. Just like Ferguson said: The bosses' real daughter comes home.

And more than that, the bosses' *famous* real daughter. Who wouldn't gawk?

The path rises a little now, and when I glance back, I can see the boat dock down by the water.

The ferry has just arrived. Three people—a man and two women—get off.

"Who are they?" I ask, pointing behind us.

Celeste squints. "Board people, but I can't tell which ones. I haven't really seen all of them close up."

"How many are there?"

"Fifteen, I think."

I can feel a nervous pit in my stomach. But I can't think about the board meeting right now. I need to face this day one challenge at a time.

"There it is," Celeste says, pointing to a long, rectangular building at the bottom of the hill. "I love it there. Don't you just love horses? Do you have any at your house?"

"No." At least I don't think Halli does. She's never mentioned them, and I didn't see any when Jake and I drove away from there.

Speaking of Jake—

He comes out of the stables, and . . .

Right. So, yeah . . .

It's just that I'm used to Will looking a certain way. Back in my world, he's usually wearing cargo shorts and a T-shirt of some kind. His black hair is usually tousled and uncombed, because he's rushed out of the house to get to school or to work. And even if he had time to shave in the morning, by afternoon there's always that beginning shadow of stubble on his beautiful, perfect face.

I've studied that face for so many years, I could draw it from memory.

So it's weird that when I see Jake, he looks so . . . not Will. More like a completely different person. Someone more rugged. More rustic.

When he came to get me at Halli's house yesterday, he'd been dressed like he was going to a job interview—nice pants, nice shirt, jacket. Then last night at dinner he was as dressed up as the rest of them there, like they were all at some formal party.

But now, standing outside the stables in his dusty, worn-out jeans, his scuffed-up boots, and plain denim shirt, with the wind messing up his hair, and that particular smile of his teasing the edges of his mouth, he looks so good I can barely stand it, and I'm having a hard time remembering why it is I'm not supposed to let him kiss me anymore.

As we get closer, I'm trying to think of what to say. How to keep it light, but professional, friendly, but not too friendly.

I end up going with "Hey."

"Miss Markham," he answers. "Don't you look nice."

And he keeps on looking at me. In that way Will never has. I swear, I would have sold all my possessions and given them to Will's charity fund on the spot if he'd only looked at me that way once. It would have stopped my heart. It's close to stopping it now.

"You look nice, too," I say in a strained voice. Then I cough and look away because I realize I've been staring at him this whole time.

Jake reaches out and bats his little sister's braid. "Celie. How's your day going?"

"Good," she says. "Can I stay? Please? Just for a while?"

"Did you ask Alexa?"

Celeste frowns. "No."

"Tell you what," Jake says. "If Miss Markham will agree to it, we'll say she asked you to stay, in case she needs anything from the house. Will that do?"

He's asking me that question. Which means he's looking at me. Again.

"Oh. Sure," I say. "Whatever." What I'm really thinking is he needs to stand further over *there*, because on top of everything else, he smells a little too nice today, even though that scent is mixed with horse. Or maybe that's what makes it so nice. It's so earthy and natural and primitive—

I take a step away. It seems like the smart thing to do.

"Are you ready to ride?" Jake asks me.

"Um, I wanted to talk to you about that," I say, turning to the lie I scripted on the way over. "I'm not really feeling up to riding today. I thought maybe we could just talk about a few things—"

"But you have to!" Celeste says. "My father will be so disappointed."

"Sorry, but I'm tired after that session with Ferguson. Maybe some other time."

"Please, Miss Halli," Celeste says.

"If she doesn't want to, she doesn't have to," Jake says. "Come on, Celie, let's give Miss Markham some room."

Yes, give Miss Markham *lots* of room. And would you please stop *looking* at her like that? The girl inside Miss Markham's body might not be handling it very well at the moment.

"Will you at least meet our father?" Jake asks me.

"Of course," I say. And even though I hear what he just said—the "our" part—I don't really *hear* it, hear it.

The two of them lead me into the stables. My eyes adjust to the lower light. And there, materializing out of the dark, is a face I almost think I know. It belongs to a dark-haired, middle-aged man who's smiling and coming toward me.

I freeze in Halli's skin.

"Halli Markham," Jake says, "meet my father, Oscar Nuñez."

"So pleased to meet you," he says, warmly grasping my hand. "You're very welcome here, Miss Markham. Very welcome."

I smile and nod bravely. And shake the hand of a dead man.

16

I wonder if anyone else can see my brain actually spinning in my head. I wonder if my eyes look at all unsteady, or if the smile frozen on my face is flickering in some way, so that any moment someone's going to ask, "Are you having a mental breakdown, Miss Markham? Can we get you anything?"

I have seen this man in photos. He's always younger, which makes sense, since HE DIED fifteen years ago.

But he didn't die—not here. Here he's lived long enough that his twin children actually know him—he's not just stories and pictures to them, but a living, breathing father.

And his widow never remarried and had a child with her new husband because there is no new husband

—this old one would do, and the two of them could make a third child together quite nicely, thank you.

I know it's all possible, in a scientific way, but it still just totally blows my mind.

I guess I haven't really examined the whole parallel universe thing—I mean, not *really*. I know there are people over here who look just like the ones I have in my world—Halli, for example, and Daniel's sister Sarah —and I know that in my universe my own copy of a grandmother is still alive even though Halli's here isn't —but still! Come on! You don't just see a dead guy come back to life every day.

"It's very nice to meet you, sir." And I mean it. I wish so much that Will and Lydia could be here. I would happily change places with them a million times over, and not just because I want to go home, but for them. It doesn't seem fair that I'm the one who gets to meet the father they never knew.

"You don't have to call me 'sir,'" he tells me. "Just 'Oscar' will do."

I swallow the glitch in my throat. "Yes, sir. I mean, Oscar. I just . . . it's just SO nice to meet you." I'm still holding his hand. With my other hand I reach up and pat him on the arm. I'm in danger of hugging the man. I'm not sure what he'll do.

Out of the corner of my eye, I see Jake watching me very closely.

I clear my throat and try to cover it up with a laugh. "Anyway." I pat Oscar Nuñez's arm one more time, and then reluctantly, I let him go.

But I wish I could take a picture. Or that I knew how to draw so I could make a sketch of him. Not that I'll ever be able to bring anything like that with me if I ever do find my way back to my own universe, but just seeing him and not being able to record it somehow for Will and Lydia seems like a horrible crime.

Or would it be even worse for them to know that their father exists, alive somewhere, and they'll never be able to reach him?

"Miss Markham?" Oscar asks. "Is everything all right?"

Okay, that does it.

"Please," I tell all of them. "From now on it's just 'Halli.' You don't have to call me Miss anything anymore. In fact, I'm begging you not to call me that—it's driving me crazy. I'm sorry, it's very nice of you, but honestly, stop."

Jake looks like he's trying not to laugh.

Celeste starts to protest. "But Dr. Markham said—"

"—that we should give Miss Markham whatever she wants," Jake finishes. "And what she wants is not to be called Miss Markham. That's easy enough."

"But I'll get in trouble," Celeste says, and I can see she's actually worried.

"You won't get in trouble," I say. "You can still call

me whatever you need to if anyone else is around. But if it's just us, you have to call me Halli. Okay?"

Celeste still isn't convinced. "But what about Alexa?"

Now it's her father's turn. "Your sister is not in charge of Miss Markham," Oscar says. "If Halli tells us we have to call her Guadalupe Candlesticks, we have to do it, don't we Miss Markham?" He winks at me.

"I thought about using that name," I say, "but Halli seemed so much easier. So. Is it settled?"

Celeste still looks unsure, but she nods. Then her father distracts her by assigning her the job of helping him pick out a horse for me.

I'm just about to tell them not to bother, when Jake comes up alongside me. He's so close our arms brush against each other. And then he leans in to whisper, and maybe it's natural that his arm loops inside mine, and his hand slides down my forearm until he ends up clasping my fingers. And maybe it's also natural that a thousand volts of electricity travel from my fingers up my arm, until they zap me square in the head.

And as if that's not bad enough, what Jake whispers to me is this: "Miss Markham, how is it possible you're even better than I ever expected?"

Forget it. Game over. Because right now my head feels like a family of bees has swarmed in through my ear, and they're so busy catching up with each other I can barely hear myself over the buzz.

And meanwhile Jake is so close to me I can almost

taste the scent of his skin—that blend of his own unique smell, mixed with a little horse sweat and fresh hay. If someone could bottle that, turn it into a bath oil or a body spray or something I could just constantly rub under my nose, I'd pay them half of whatever I earn for the rest of my life.

We're standing there like that, hands clasped together, leaning lightly against each other, so cozy it's like we've been doing it all our lives, when this persistent, annoying, *irritating* thought keeps poking at my brain. Trying to get my attention. I ignore it, but it just won't leave me alone. So finally I have to turn to it and say, *"What?"*

"Psst," it answers back. *"He thinks you're Halli. Not you —remember?"*

Oh. Right. That.

Which is also the reason I should be thinking only of Daniel Everett right now. Because he likes me—the real me—the sciency, universe-hopping, non-sporty me. He actually prefers that girl over Halli—he made a point once of telling me so.

He also made a point of telling me he'll be waiting for me, hoping I'll figure out the physics of our parallel universes, so we can spend more time together in the future. He said he'll be looking for me—not Halli, me.

So that's where my loyalty should lie. No question. Which means there's only one thing to do.

Even though it's going to take a superhuman force of will to do it.

"Come on," I say, pulling my hand out of Jake's and stepping away from him. "I need to talk to you. In private. I don't have much time. Let's hurry up and get this over with."

17

"How much farther is it?" I ask. We've been hiking up this mountain behind the mansion for a while. It's a little mountain, compared to any of the ones Halli and I hiked in the Alps, but it still takes time to climb.

And now I really wish I were wearing her hiking boots instead of these slippery, pointy cowgirl ones.

"If you wanted to go faster," Jake says, "we could have taken the horses."

"Yeah, well, maybe next time."

I'm pretty sure Red is happy we didn't. I noticed he didn't come into the stable with me. And when I came back out on foot, he seemed pretty eager to follow Jake and me into the forest to see what adventure we were up to next.

But Jake hasn't thrown him a stick once, and this isn't one of those leisurely strolls like we had along the beach, and then through the woods last night. This is a march. Not that I mind it, but I just don't see the point.

"Are you telling me people can hear us here in the woods?" I ask. "Do we really have to keep going?"

"You wanted me to take you somewhere private," Jake says. "I'm taking you somewhere private."

He keeps hauling himself up the hillside. Fine—I've got the legs for that.

When we finally crest the ridge on top, I have to pause a moment to take it all in. It's spectacular—the view of the water, the nearby islands, the real mountains off in the distance. And even the landing strip where the pilot landed our jet yesterday afternoon.

And something else.

I can see the boat dock. The ferry has just pulled up to it, and some people are getting off. More board members, I'd guess.

"Do you know those people?" I ask Jake.

"Don't you?" he answers.

"You know I don't. Ginny never told me."

"Well, you'll find out," he says.

Not exactly the chatty, helpful, informative guy he was last night. And I'm pretty sure I know why.

I've been pretty cold to him the whole way up this hill, and I feel bad about that, but it's for the greater good. I can see he's confused by my change of personality, but you should just get used to that when you're dealing with a body-snatching girl from another universe. You never know what she'll do next.

I clear away some twigs and rocks to make a place for myself to sit down. Red has already dug himself a bed and is enjoying a nap in the sun. I really admired that about him in the Alps, too—his ability to turn the switch to off the minute we stopped to take a break. I think that's a good skill. I might need to learn it.

Jake takes a seat a little ways away from me in the dirt. He picks up a long thin stick and starts snapping it into little pieces.

We both stare out at the ocean.

"Okay, look," I say. "I'm going to ask you for a favor. You don't have to do it, obviously, but I really hope you will. It's very, very important to me, and the sooner I can get this information, the better."

Jake snaps another twig.

"It's about my tracking," I say.

He pauses, then goes back to breaking his stick.

"I know my parents saw it," I continue, "since they knew when to send you, but did you look at it, too?"

"Maybe."

That's not the answer I'm expecting. "What do you mean, maybe?"

Now Jake turns to me. "What's going on, Halli? Or should I go back to calling you Miss Markham?"

"Maybe you should," I say. "And I'd like you to

answer my question. You won't get in trouble—I won't tell anyone. I just need the information."

He vaults to his feet and starts pacing.

"Did I do something?" he wants to know. "Did I offend you somehow? I'm sorry about last night—I thought . . . well, I thought maybe you wanted that, too. But obviously I was wrong."

I want *so* much to tell him he wasn't, but I have to stay strong. I press my lips together to keep them from blurting out the way I really feel.

"It was a mistake," Jake says. "So I'm sorry. But you had no reason to take it out on my father and dismiss him the way you did—"

"I didn't dismiss him!"

"He spent all morning grooming those horses," Jake says. "Raking out the stalls. Shining every buckle, rubbing down every saddle. He was so honored he might get to meet you. He's been talking about it for a week."

A lump pops up in my throat.

"I'm sorry," I say. "I never meant to offend your father. He's a wonderful man. I was very happy to meet him. You have no idea."

"No, I don't have any idea," Jake says. "One minute you were friendly with all of us, and the next you're telling my sister to go back to the house and ordering me to come speak with you—"

"I didn't order you! I asked."

"When Miss Markham makes a request," Jake says sarcastically, "every knee must bow. Isn't that what you're used to out there? I was afraid you'd be just like your parents. Now I see I was right."

I growl in frustration. "It's not like that! *I'm* not like that."

And neither is the real Halli, I want to say. I've seen her have to deal with being a celebrity, but she was never arrogant about it. She never expected people to bow to her. If people wanted to act like she was royalty, that was their choice, not hers. All that attention seemed to wear her out.

"Then what are you like?" Jake asks. "Because I can't figure it out."

I'm glad that Ferguson isn't here to see me misusing Halli's body again. My shoulders slump. I curl over and hug my knees. This whole thing is going to be harder than I thought.

"Jake . . ."

He stands there looking at me, waiting.

I pat the dirt next to me. "Sit back down. I'll try to tell you the truth."

18

The truth is relative. I think maybe Albert Einstein said that. If not, he should have.

I actually gave it some thought as we hiked up the mountain, because I was afraid it might come to this. And even though Celeste bought my lame excuse that I wasn't used to that newer model of tablet, I had the feeling Jake would probably need a more substantial explanation. Meaning a more substantial lie.

So I give it a try.

"You can't tell anyone what I'm about to tell you," I start out. "Please—first I need you to promise me that."

He hesitates, but then nods.

I take a breath. "Okay, so I had an accident. In the Alps. I was climbing where I shouldn't have—it was really stupid—and there was a rock slide. I got hit in the head. Passed out. It was pretty scary when I woke up."

Jake's expression has changed. He doesn't seem so angry anymore. But he also doesn't seem entirely convinced.

"I've lost time," I tell him. "I don't even know how much of it. There are these gaps in my memory, and I don't know how else to fill them in. I'm hoping you can help me find my tracking information so maybe I can retrace what happened."

"When?" Jake asks.

"When did it happen? Pretty close to the end of my trip." I haven't thought of which specific day to say it occurred, but a general answer seems good enough.

"Which parts don't you remember?" he asks.

"I . . . I'm not really sure how I got home. To Colorado. That's all kind of a blank."

Jake runs his hand through his hair. "Halli . . ."

"I know," I say. "It's pretty bad."

"Have you seen a doctor?" he asks.

"No. I feel fine except for . . . that."

"We have a doctor here on the island—"

"No," I say. "That won't work. I can't let my parents know."

"Why?"

Good question. I haven't really thought that far through.

Luckily Jake is already on to his next concern.

"Why didn't you just look up the information yourself?"

Another good question, but this time I have an answer.

"Because that's another thing I've lost," I say. "I can't remember my code."

"Halli, you *have* to see a doctor."

"What I need," I say, "is to know what happened. If you can help me with that—please."

"Of course I'll help you," he says. "But then you've got to see a doctor. It doesn't have to be the one here, but I'm not letting you go home until someone looks at your head. Do you understand?"

That's not a bargain I'm willing to make, but I don't tell him that. I don't tell him that the real problem isn't in my head, it's in the physics. That I've lost time not because I have selective amnesia, but because I violated the natural order of the universe. And that finding out what happened in those minutes before and after the event might help me to unravel the whole sequence, so that maybe I'll have even the remotest chance of repairing what I've done.

Jake is on his feet again, pacing.

"What's the last thing you remember?" he asks. "Which day?"

"Tuesday, I think."

"Tuesday you were in Munich," Jake says.

"Munich? No . . ." On Tuesday Halli was still in the Alps, about to be killed by an avalanche.

"You were staying at your grandmother's apartment there," Jake says. "Don't you remember?"

"But . . . that's impossible."

"Why is it impossible?" he asks.

"Because . . ." I quickly improvise. "Tuesday is when I hit my head. That's when the rock slide was."

"Halli, look at me." Now Jake really sounds worried. I'm starting to feel worried myself. "I watched your dot. You were in Munich. You arrived there Sunday night. You didn't leave until Wednesday morning, when you caught your flight home."

That's all impossible. He has to be wrong.

"Jake, are you absolutely sure? This is important."

"I know it's important," he says. "Yes, I'm sure."

Now my head is really reeling. It means I've lost not just two days from Halli's life, but four.

But how is that possible? I clearly remember saying goodbye to Halli in the Alps on Sunday morning, and watching her walk away to go join that guy Karl, the German pilot, for another few days of hiking. Then I clearly remember seeing her again some time on Tuesday, when I did that remote viewing exercise in Professor Whitfield's lab. I saw Karl being buried in the avalanche, and then Halli and Red in its pathway to be next.

But did I make that part of it up? Has my brain lied to me?

But how could it? Isn't the evidence right here? I, Audie Masters, am no longer in my own body, in my own universe. That is a verifiable fact. My brain is not imagining that I am stuck here in Halli's body, in Halli's world. I am the living, physical proof that what I remember happening, happened.

But then, how can what Jake said be true?

I cradle my head in my hands. This is all too much to take.

Jake pries away one of my hands. "Halli, look at me."

I gaze up at him with tear-fogged eyes. He has no idea how much I wish this were all a dream.

"I'm going to help you," he tells me. "Whatever you need. I promise, you're going to be all right."

I don't have the heart to tell him that promise isn't within his power to make.

19

"Lyman, can you find Celeste for me and ask her to come to my room?"

"Certainly, Miss Markham."

Yes, I could ask for Celeste through the walls, but there's no way I want Alexa to know anything that I'm up to.

Because there's one possible person who might be able to shed some light on Halli's last few days, and that's Daniel. On Sunday, when Halli supposedly left the Alps and traveled back to Munich, Daniel and his sister Sarah and their friend Martin were also leaving the Alps to go back home to London.

If Halli hiked out with them, Daniel can tell me.

Not that that solves any of the mystery of what happened and why my memory is so different from

Halli's tracking information, but at least it's something. At least it's a fact. Right now I need every fact I can find.

I pace back and forth until there's a knock on my door. I rush to open it, then greet Celeste with my finger to my lips. I motion for her to follow me to the closet.

"I need a huge favor," I tell her as soon as we're inside.

She answers with a nod.

But she's not smiling. She's not bubbly or exuberant or enthusiastic, like she's been every other time we're together.

Clearly Jake was right.

"Celeste, I'm so sorry if I hurt your feelings earlier. That's the last thing I wanted to do. You're one of my favorite people here—I hope you know that."

I can see her softening.

"I've been really worried about something," I go on, "but I'm sorry if I took it out on you. I just needed to talk to your brother right away, and I probably seemed pretty rude."

"No, it's all right . . ."

"It's not all right, and I'm sorry. Please, let's be friends."

I offer her my hand, and she shakes it. Then she gives me a little of her normal smile.

"You didn't fight," she asks, "did you?"

"Who, me and Jake? Not at all. We're fine. But now I need to ask you a favor, and you can't tell him anything about it. Please. I need you to promise."

"Why?" I can tell she doesn't like the sound of any of it.

"Because he might not understand," I say, "and I don't want to hurt his feelings, either. I need to contact somebody—a guy I know—but he's just a friend—really, the brother of a friend of mine—and I don't want Jake to find out about it and assume the wrong thing. Do you understand?"

"Yes . . ." But she doesn't look very happy about it.

"Please, Celeste. I promise it's nothing bad. I just need to talk to this person to ask him something. So will you help me?"

"Yes, Miss, I'll help you."

"It's still Halli," I remind her. "I meant that."

"Yes, all right." But she still seems guarded and concerned.

I hand her the tablet. "Can you find this person for me? His name is Daniel Everett. He lives in England—in London, I think."

She works on the tablet until a cube rotates above it. Then the cube dissolves into a face I instantly recognize.

It's just a 3-D image of him, but seeing Daniel here, so close to me, feels like such a comfort. There's his brownish-blond hair, his light brown eyes, his kind smile—

Celeste is studying him, too. Because despite what I said, she must realize he's a potential rival for her brother. The girl isn't stupid.

"Is that all?" she asks.

"Yes. Thank you." I reach over and squeeze her hand. "Seriously, Celeste, thank you for everything you've helped me with. You don't know how much I appreciate it."

"He's nice looking," she says, gesturing toward Daniel's head.

"He's a nice guy. So is his sister. She's a lot of fun—I bet you'd like her."

Better to emphasize Sarah more than Daniel. Keep the focus off of him.

I have Celeste show me where to press on the tablet to connect the comm, and she's just about to leave when a horrible thought occurs to me. I'm almost afraid to ask, because if she answers the wrong way, my life is only going to get more complicated.

"Whose tablet is this, Celeste?"

"It's for the guests," she says.

"Yes, but whose is it, exactly? Is it Alexa's?"

"No, it's not really anybody's," she says. "It just belongs to the house. Anyone who stays here can borrow it."

I'm thinking of the walls outside the closet. And the

fact that they were built in such a way that someone from Halli's parents' staff can listen in to whatever's being said. Of course it's only for the guest's convenience—I can imagine that's what they'd say.

And if there's something "convenient" like that built into this tablet—

"Does anybody monitor this?" I ask. "You know, like could someone find out who I contacted with it?" Or even worse, "Can anybody listen in to what I'm saying on it?"

Celeste looks uncomfortable. "Yes."

"Who? Alexa?"

"No, only Dr. Markham or Dr. Bellows. I think."

Great.

There go my dreams for an honest, heart-to-heart chat with Daniel where I tell him everything that's happened in the past two days, and ask him to try to help me figure out what in the world happened to Halli.

"Thank you, Celeste. That's all I need right now. I'll see you later."

I wait until she leaves to slump back against the wall.

This island of Halli's parents might be beautiful, but it's a prison.

Now what am I supposed to do?

20

I have to at least try. So I press where Celeste showed me to press.

It takes a minute or so, but then the lights swirling above the tablet form into a face, and that face is speaking to me.

"Halli!"

I smile so wide it feels like this might be my first real smile since I took over this body.

"Hi, Daniel! How are you?" I say it as warmly, as personally as I can. *Please, secretly know it's me.*

"Splendid," he answers, as only a British guy can get away with. "Is Audie there with you?"

I wish he hadn't said my name, but I can't shush him without drawing further attention to it.

"Um, not right now," I say. "Listen, I just have a quick question for you."

"And I have one for you," he says. "Are you coming to my father's party?"

His father's 50th birthday party. While back in my world Gemma's family is planning a formal ball for their father, Daniel and Sarah and their version of that family here are hosting a much more modest event. And they've invited Halli and me to attend.

"Um, when is it?" I ask, just to be polite. I seriously doubt I'll be flying over to London to attend some party, when I have much more serious matters to attend to here.

"Next Saturday," he says. "My parents would love to meet you two. And Sarah—well, you can imagine how happy she'd be if you came."

Actually, I can. Sarah Everett may be the biggest Halli Markham fan I've met yet.

"I'll try," I say. "Listen, Daniel, I just need to know one thing."

I've thought about what I'm going to say. How best to frame the question so Daniel won't think it's weird, and ask a bunch of follow-up questions, and Halli's parents, if they're listening in, won't get suspicious.

"Do you remember about what time it was when we started hiking out of the Alps?"

The "we" is the key. If Halli didn't go with him, he'll

say so in some way, like, "I don't know what time you left, but we left at X." I'm hoping.

"It was early," he says. "Wasn't it around seven?"

My heart pounds. Was that answer enough? Does that mean for sure that Halli was with him?

I need to ask one more question. My voice is shaking a little. I wonder if Daniel notices.

"And about what time was it when we all separated —do you remember?"

I remember it clearly. It was early in the morning—7:00 might be right—and Daniel and Sarah and Martin hiked off down a trail that would lead them to the lake at the bottom. Then they were going to catch a boat that would take them to the nearest town where they could take a train back home.

Halli and I waited there at the trailhead a few minutes more, watching them go, then she and I walked off together toward the hut where everyone had been staying. Then she took off with Karl, and I brought myself back to my own universe, back to Professor Whitfield's lab.

I have absolutely no doubt that's exactly how it happened.

But Daniel remembers it differently.

"I believe it was close to four," he says. "We were worried we might miss the ferry—remember? You thought they might have cancelled the last few runs because of the snow. But we caught the three o'clock, then ended at the train station around four. Does that sound right?"

My mouth is dirt dry. "Yes. Exactly."

"Why do you ask?" Daniel wants to know.

"I just . . . I was curious. I couldn't remember, and it was bothering me."

My stomach feels like it's flipped over and is lying on its side. I clutch it to try to hold it in place.

"Okay, thanks, Daniel." I don't know what else to say. This was my one last hope that what Jake told me was wrong. Now I know all the wrongness is in me.

"How is Audie?" he asks. "Any chance I can speak with her?"

He understands the complications of my life. Or did understand them, as they were just a week or so ago— me showing up and disappearing at random, me trying to learn to control where I ended up in this universe, and for how long.

Those days seem so easy to me now. At least I had Halli to help me. At least I thought I was learning the rules.

But what are the rules now? I can't rely on my brain anymore—not if it could be so wrong about what it remembers—and I have no power over where I go or when I leave. I'm completely body-bound right now, stuck doing whatever Halli's physical form is capable of. Granted, that's more than my own, much less burly, body at home can do, but it's not like I can hop back and forth between universes anymore, and sleep in my own bed every night.

Not to mention in my own body.

"I miss you," I tell Daniel, before realizing I've just said it. I slap my hand over my mouth.

Daniel looks surprised. I don't blame him. Halli was never that emotive with him in person.

"Yes, well, it would be wonderful to see the two of you," he answers in his proper British way. "Please try to come. If there's anything I can do to help . . ."

I shake my head no. I don't trust myself to speak anymore. There's so much I want to say, and it all has to stay unsaid.

I wave to him—*wave* to him. How's that for a goodbye?

I don't know how to turn off the call, so I just have to leave Daniel's head still floating there in the dark while I open the closet door and get out.

"Miss Markham," says the person who was obviously listening on the other side. "If I might have a word with you."

21

I'm so startled to see Alexa standing there, I don't have time to get back into character. She may think she's looking at Halli Markham, but the girl she's talking to is all me.

"Wh-what?" I say, looking back guiltily at the closet. I wonder what she heard.

"It's three-thirty," she says. "The meeting begins in half an hour. Your mother has instructed me to escort you to the conference room. Some of the board members are quite anxious to meet you. We'll have to do something about your dog, as well."

"The dog stays with me."

"Your mother insists that—"

"I don't care what she insists," I say, feeling the

return of some of the courage I had this morning. "The dog comes with me, or I'm not going."

I can see Alexa's jawline tighten. She's obviously clenching her teeth.

But she smiles nevertheless. "Of course, Miss Markham," she says with sickening sweetness. "Whatever you say. You can take it up directly with Dr. Markham."

"I'd be happy to," I say. "Let's go."

I'm ready to follow Alexa out the door, but she hasn't moved yet. She casts a scornful look at my clothes.

"You still have time to change," she says.

"I've changed enough already," I tell her, which might be the most honest thing I've said since I stepped foot on this place.

22

So I'm still dressed as a cowgirl. Except I did take a minute to change out of the Western boots, back into Halli's comfortable hiking ones. I feel like I need the support right now. The more of Halli I bring with me, the better.

The conference room is another holographic nightmare. Instead of normal, solid walls, the whole place is an ever-moving, constantly-changing sequence of different outdoor locations, all captioned with the company logo: OPS Chile . . . OPS England . . . OPS Finland, France, Iceland, India . . .

As my eyes adjust to the light, I see that all conversation has stopped, and about twenty or more people are all staring right at me. Then some of them smile. And some of them don't.

"Here she is!" Halli's mother calls out. "Our daughter."

In what might be the friendliest tone I've ever heard from her.

"Back from her latest exciting adventure," Halli's father says in a jovial voice. "Climbing the Alps this time!"

Then the two of them lead the room in a round of applause.

While I stand here completely shocked.

"This is your first time here, isn't it, Miss Markham?" some guy asks. He's looking through what looks like giant, square binoculars. "First time at your parents' headquarters?"

"Uh . . . yes," I say, glancing at Halli's parents for confirmation. They're both still smiling in this weird, frozen way.

The guy tilts the binoculars down. "And this is the dog? Red, is it?"

I step closer to the Lab so I can feel his body against my leg. I don't know if it's for his protection, or mine. I rest my hand on his head. "Yes. Red."

The binoculars tilt back up to my face. "What's next for Halli Markham?" the guy asks in this kind of fake, announcer's voice.

And finally I realize what's going on: this must be the history reporter Alexa mentioned this morning.

Which might explain Halli's parents' bizarre transformation. They want to look good in front of the media. And maybe in front of the board members, too.

So I have two choices: I can go along with it, or I can resist.

And I don't know what it is—maybe some instinct inside me, maybe some instant perception that playing along with Halli's parents right now could bring me some advantage in the future. Maybe I'm wrong about that, but I decide to trust my gut.

"I'm just enjoying my time with my parents right now," I tell the reporter. "I don't know what I'm doing next. I like to focus on the moment."

Out of the corner of my eye, I see Halli's mother relax.

The reporter laughs in this fakey, newscaster way. "Well, as always, we'll be watching and looking forward to your next adventure!"

Then he lowers the binoculars and says in a normal voice, "That'll do. Thanks for your time, Miss Markham. Nice to see you again."

"Yeah," I say, "you, too." Please don't let him get more specific than that.

The reporter starts to wander away, when a heavy-set man breaks from his group and starts heading toward me. On the way, he motions for the reporter to lift his camera again and keep filming.

"Miss Markham, Miss Markham!" the man says. He

has a pleasant-enough grin beneath his thick, walrusy mustache. "So wonderful to finally meet you!"

He reaches out to shake my hand, without bothering to introduce himself.

"And this is the famous pooch!" he says, patting Red on the head. The dog answers with a low growl.

"I wish my wife could have come," the man chatters on. "She's been talking about you for years! Made our daughters watch the histories of you and your grandmother practically from the day they were born." He chuckles to himself. "Always said she wanted to raise them wild just like you. My youngest, Becca, says she wants to move to Africa and live with the gorillas. I'll have you to thank if she runs away to do just that!"

He laughs again, then shakes my hand one more time. "Good to meet you, good to meet you. If you don't mind—"

He turns to make sure we're both facing the reporter. Then he throws his arm across my shoulder. "Can you say hi to Becca, Shannon, and my wife Michelle? I know they'd be thrilled."

"Hi . . ." I look to him to repeat the names. Once he does, I smile and recite them in Halli's friendliest way. "Hi, Becca, Shannon, and Michelle. So glad to meet you. It was nice meeting your dad and husband. Bye, now."

I hope that was good enough, but even if it's not, that's all I have. Because I notice Jake is finally free from the conversation he was having with Halli's father and some other man, and now he's heading this way.

I'm not sure what to tell him. There's no point in saying I've just confirmed that what he saw on Halli's tracking was, apparently, correct. He'd have no reason to doubt it anyway.

And since he's now all hot on the idea of me getting my head examined, I don't know what to say other than that I feel fine and I wish this meeting were already over. I'm not looking forward to anyone saying, "And what do you think, Miss Markham?" and me saying, "Umm . . . ."

But I'm spared improvising with Jake, because another one of the board members is clearly making her way towards me.

She's a delicate, white-haired woman who looks like she's about eighty years old. She's small—about a foot shorter than Halli—and she walks with a surprising amount of energy. As she draws closer she gazes up at me with her bright blue eyes and gives me a smile that instantly sets me at ease.

"Halli, dear," she says in a gentle, British accent. She takes my hand between her soft, bony ones. Her skin is pleasantly warm.

"Mrs. Scott," the reporter says, binoculars back to his face.

"Not now," she answers, waving him away. "This is private, Bryan."

"Yes, ma'am." He drifts off to interview other people.

The woman pats my hand. "I haven't seen you since you were a little, little girl. You probably don't remember me?"

"No, ma'am, I'm sorry."

"Don't be sorry, dear! I wouldn't expect you to know —you were very, very small. My name is Lillian Scott. I was a great admirer of your grandmother's. I was so sorry to hear of her passing—she was genuinely one of a kind."

"Yes, ma'am, she was."

"Come closer, dear," she whispers.

I bend toward her.

"I want you to know that I support you in this," she says, patting my hand again. "You can count on me. I won't let them get away with it."

Excuse me? Get away with *what*?

23

Before I can ask Mrs. Scott what she means, Halli's father calls out over the crowd, "Everyone take their seats. Monsieur Bern has arrived."

There's a swirl of lights rising above a tablet sitting on the long conference table. Soon the lights collect themselves into a face.

He's about Halli's parents' age, with blond hair in a very square cut, right down to the straight line of bangs. He has round, gold-framed glasses, and a small, thin mouth.

"Shall we begin?" Halli's father says. People murmur and settle in.

Nobody tells me where I should sit, so I grab one of the seats at the furthest end of the table. Red settles in at my feet. The man closest to me looks over, meets my eye, then pointedly turns away and ignores me.

So this should all be fun.

The lights dim, and the holographic walls disappear. In their place is a 3-D movie surrounding us on every side.

"Osmotic Power Systems," a female voice says. "London . . . Paris . . . Santiago . . . Seattle . . ."

A different set of buildings pops up for each location. Different scenery in the background of each.

" . . . Sydney . . . Toronto . . ." Several more cities and buildings before she gets to the end.

Then a man, in the lobby of some building, walking toward the camera with a cup of liquid in his hand.

"Water," he says dramatically. "It can change the world. From bringing power to a desperate city—"

Cut to a view of whatever desperate city he's talking about.

"—to lighting up a school house—"

A group of shabbily-dressed kids, smiling as they listen to their teacher.

"—to powering the life-saving equipment at this remote hospital."

A group of doctors and nurses having a serious discussion in a hospital hallway, with patients being wheeled past them.

"But here at OPS," the man says, "good enough is

never good enough. We pride ourselves on innovation—"

Cut to some huge, complicated-looking set of pipes and tubes.

"—conservation—"

Tweeting birds and a lush green jungle.

"—and preservation."

A large blue lake, surrounded by forest.

"And that's why we asked ourselves—"

Back to the man in the lobby, holding up his cup of liquid.

"'What can we do with just one cup?'"

Now there are cars streaming down a highway, in that same steady configuration I saw when Jake took me to the airport: all the cars evenly spaced, no rushing, no passing. As the camera zooms in, I can see drivers sitting in their cars reading or working on their tablets, facing and talking with their passengers—even a woman changing her baby's diaper right there in the front seat. No one is paying attention to the road.

"Just one cup," the man says again, and now there's an airplane flying through the clouds. "One cup to take you from New York to London. One cup from Helsinki to Singapore.

"One cup to power our lives," he concludes. "One cup to change the world."

And now back to the OPS logo, and the woman's voice from the beginning.

"Osmotic Power Systems," she says soothingly. "Changing the world, one drop of water at a time."

The lights come up. And the walls are a simple beige.

"You've all had a chance to read the materials on our hydro-catalytic process," Halli's father says. It's a statement, not a question. "I've brought in Dr. Brubaker here and Mr. Lindstrom to answer any questions you have about either the process or the economics. But we're hoping to move through this meeting today and reach a conclusion by the end of it.

"Does anyone have any questions for our experts?" Halli's father asks the group.

Mrs. Scott raises her hand. "I have a question for you, Jameson," she answers him. "I'm certain we would all like to hear why we're in such a grand *rush* all of a sudden. This technology of yours has been on the horizon for years."

She glances at me. And gives me a slight nod.

"Circumstances continue to develop," Halli's father says. "We could continue to delay, but the split-off of the hydro-catalytic division is inevitable. And that will require a restructuring of the company. Which makes this an appropriate time to address the buy-out of Virginia's old shares. Better to take care of it all now rather than six months from now, when it might be even more complicated."

"But we're not speaking of six months, are we?"

Mrs. Scott says. "Merely four, when your daughter turns eighteen. Then she can vote on this matter herself."

"I am her trustee," Monsieur Bern interjects. His accent sounds French. "Virginia Markham appointed me to act on Mademoiselle Markham's behalf until she is of age. I have reviewed the proposal, and assured myself it is in the best interests of the child. We may proceed with an agreement. There is no need for delay."

I am sitting desperately still, trying to capture all this with my ears. I've never heard *any* of this—not about Ginny owning shares in this company, not about Halli having a trustee, not about her having some interest in her parents' company that would require her to vote on something—none of it.

But suddenly something makes sense: Jake never finished telling me the story of Ginny's history with Halli's parents. We were too busy kissing. But I'll bet if I'd never gotten cold hands and Jake hadn't had to wrap me in his coat and we hadn't ended up making out as a result—I'll bet if none of that had happened, he might have gotten to the point in the story where he told me Halli's grandmother owned some interest in the company in exchange for the money she gave Halli's parents.

And now Halli owns it. She told me that Ginny left her all her houses and apartments all over the world, so why wouldn't Ginny have left her whatever shares she owned in this company, too? It's all starting to make sense. And I just have to sit here and act calm.

But now I get it! Monsieur Bern is here because Halli was underage when she inherited. So he gets to act on her behalf until she turns eighteen. But after that, Halli gets to decide everything herself.

Which means I have a responsibility here. I have to do whatever I can to make sure I don't leave Halli worse off than before. I don't know what she would have said about any of this, but I can't take the chance of making a mistake that she can't undo.

Because I intend to bring her back. Until then, I'm just a placeholder in her life.

"Can I say something?" I ask. My voice sounds tiny and hoarse. But Mrs. Scott gazes at me with those clear blue eyes of hers and encourages me with a smile.

Be Halli, be Halli, be Halli . . .

"I agree with Mrs. Scott," I say. "I'm not ready to vote. I need to think about it for a while."

"*Think* about it?" Halli's father says with a laugh. "What's there to think about? You've never thought about this company one second of your life—neither did your grandmother. Your mother and I have done all the work, while the two of you have been living off us all these years, doing anything you please, leading some ridiculous life—"

"Jim," Halli's mother murmurs. She tilts her head toward the reporter who's still in here filming.

"Bryan," Halli's father says to him. "You can go. I'll call you back if we need you."

I see the reporter named Bryan smile. To himself, not to Halli's father. He knows a good story when he sees one. He takes his time getting to the door.

"And it's not your decision to make," Halli's father tells me. "You have a trustee, and it's his vote that counts."

"Then why am I here?" I ask. I can't believe I'm standing up to Halli's father—he's one of the scariest men I've ever met, even if he does look like my own dad. But I can't let him intimidate me. I can't let him do something Halli might regret forever.

And if Mrs. Scott is against it, it has to be wrong. Out of all the people in this room, she's the only one it seems like I can trust.

Her and Jake. And he's not saying anything. I caught his eye just now, but I can't tell anything from his expression—not whether I'm doing the right thing or the wrong thing. I just have to go with my gut.

"I call for a vote," Halli's father says. "And you, young lady, can *leave*."

24

I t could be my ticket out.

I could storm out of this room right now, ask Lyman to arrange for the ferry, ask him to find Halli's parents' pilot, too, so I can fly back home tonight.

My priority is finding Halli, not fighting with her parents over whatever it is they want to do with their stupid company.

But flying back to Halli's house won't really get me where I need to be. There's nothing there for me right now except solitude and space to think.

And a day ago, I would have thought both of those were the most precious things in the world. But now I know differently.

Because I'm not ready to think yet—not without more facts. This is a physics problem, and you can't solve those with only part of the information. I need to understand the whole picture. And for that I need more facts.

I know where to find them. And that's not at Halli's house.

"I'm sorry," I tell Halli's father. "You're right. You're absolutely right."

"About . . . what?" her mother asks. She glances at Halli's father. Both of them look worried.

"I've completely neglected this company," I say. "You're right—Ginny and I have been busy all these years —too busy to stop and pay attention to what you were doing. But that's changed now. I don't know what the future holds for me, but I'm willing to take the time now to learn all about what you're doing. I bet it's really great."

I stop talking and hold my breath. And study Halli's parents' faces.

Because I've clearly put them on the spot. They're here in front of the board of directors of their company, with some history reporter in the room, and their long-lost daughter has just told them she wants to be part of their lives. What are they going to say—no?

I'm sure in private, they would. They don't like Halli any more than she likes them. And I'm sure they have no desire to see her involved in any way with a company they've built up from the ground.

But we're not in private, are we? And I realize that's

the whole point of why they brought me here. It's all a big act. It's all a big show. They wanted Halli to smile for the camera, smile for the board, and prove to everyone that Halli's parents were treating her fairly—that Halli was fine with the whole thing.

And at the end of the day, Monsieur Bern was going to vote the way Halli's parents wanted. Then they'd send Halli home and never speak to her again.

Which would probably suit Halli fine, but it doesn't suit me fine. Not if there's something fishy about this whole deal.

"Well," Halli's father says, clearing his throat, "it's a little late for you to try to become involved now. All these people have flown in for this meeting—"

"I don't mind," Mrs. Scott says. "Do you mind, Jeffrey?"

A man sitting across from her gives a half-hearted shrug. "As long as I can go back tonight . . ."

"Just give me a month," I tell Halli's parents, making this whole thing up as I go along. "Let me learn what you're doing, talk to some people—maybe even visit some of your other locations so I can really understand—and then we can all meet back here in a month and do the vote for real."

I decide to ask for just one month instead of four, so Halli's parents don't think I'm trying to trick them into waiting until she's eighteen. And if everything goes right, I won't even need a month, I hope—maybe just a week or so, tops.

Because what I really want is what I asked for in the middle: to go visit some of their other locations. One location, in particular.

"As I said," Halli's father answers, "whether it's today or a month from now, Monsieur Bern is the one with the power to vote your shares. And any further delay could harm the company. We need to reach a resolution today. That's why everyone is here. I call for the vote—"

"But don't you think Ginny would want me to understand what's going on?" I ask. "Even though I'm still young?" I turn to Mrs. Scott. "Do you think my grandmother would have wanted that?"

"Oh, yes, dear," she says, her eyes bright. I can see she loves that I'm in the game. "Virginia thought the sun, moon, and stars of you. I know she'd always want you to be treated fairly—especially by your parents. And I'm *certain* that if she believed the trustee she appointed wasn't adhering to your wishes, she'd see to it that he was fired and replaced immediately."

"Madame Scott," Monsieur Bern says. "If you are suggesting—"

"Let the child have her month," Mrs. Scott tells him and the rest of the board. "There's no harm in that. Miss Markham is still recovering from the death of her grandmother. I think we can all give her time."

I can see some of the board members nodding at

that. A few of them look at me sympathetically. A few won't meet my eye.

"Yes, well, thank you as always for your opinion, Lillian," Halli's father says, "but nevertheless I call for the vote. All in favor of creating a privately-owned subsidiary for the hydro-catalytic system and completing a buy-out of Virginia Markham's shares—"

"*Halli* Markham's shares," Mrs. Scott corrects him.

Halli's father pretends to ignore her. "Say 'aye.'"

"Aye."

"Aye."

But then the "no" votes start coming in.

And in the end, it's only Monsieur Bern, Halli's parents, the walrus-mustached man, Admiral Binghamton, and one other person who vote yes to Halli's father's plan.

Apparently that's not enough.

"This is unreasonable!" Halli's father says, slamming his hand on the table. "The board has all the information it needs. There's no reason for delay. What my daughter wishes or doesn't wish has no bearing on the workings of this company. She is a minority shareholder."

"Forty-nine percent is a strong minority," the man called Jeffrey answers. "If Miss Markham wants more time, I'm willing to allow her more time."

Forty-nine percent? Halli owns almost *half* of her

parents' incredibly massive, successful, international company?

Hold *on*.

My brain is careening off the wall of my skull again, and as usual I have to act totally fine. But I take a brief moment to close my eyes and do a little math.

Which I'm not normally great at, but the math here is easy: Halli must be a millionaire. Maybe even a *billionaire*, depending on how much money this company is worth. It would be like owning almost half of a giant software business, or some huge social networking company on the Internet. She might be worth more money than I've ever even imagined in my life.

Why on earth didn't Jake tell me that? I can understand that we got a little distracted last night, but he was with me all that time today, and it never came up? "Hey, by the way—everything you see on this island? You own nearly half of it."

I don't know, maybe he thought I already knew. But he knows I don't know this stuff! That's why he was filling me in on the whole history between Halli's parents and her grandmother in the first place.

And then I realize it's because of my stupid head— and the big fat lie I told about it. Once he got over being mad at me, we were already straight into the story of the imaginary rock slide and my imaginary amnesia. He was all wrapped up in my health, and forgot the part about how I could just buy the next hospital I see and ask them to treat me there.

"All in favor of a month's delay?" Mrs. Scott asks the group.

The board votes again, and the majority agrees.

"This meeting is adjourned," Halli's father says, slamming his hand again. "What a waste of everyone's time."

I look around the room, a little stunned. Halli's father is already on his feet, striding out of the room. Halli's mother is deep in conversation with Admiral Binghamton and the two experts Halli's father pointed out at the beginning. Jake and Alexa are standing at the periphery of that huddle, both of them listening in.

And Mrs. Scott is smiling at me.

I'm not exactly sure what I just did.

But I sure hope it was right.

2 5

"That was exciting, wasn't it?" Mrs. Scott whispers to me, her eyes bright. "Oh, how I wish your grandmother could have been here herself! She loved a good fight with your parents."

Jake is still over in the corner with the group of people talking to Halli's mother, but finally at least we make eye contact. He scratches the side of his cheek, then holds up that finger in what I think is a sign to wait for him. He doesn't have to worry about that—I'm dying to find out what he thought of the whole meeting.

But meanwhile I have Mrs. Scott to ask.

"Can you explain what just happened?" I ask her. "What exactly were they trying to do?"

"Cheat you, of course."

"But how?"

"By selling the company right from under you," she says. "Selling it to themselves so they can finally be rid of Virginia's shares. They only have until your birthday to do it, so I knew they'd be desperate. And that Monsieur Bern—your grandmother obviously made a mistake trusting him. But you see," she adds with a gleam in her eye, "I like a good fight, too!"

"Thank you," I tell her. "I really appreciate your support."

"You can always count on me, dear."

I'm hoping that's true. Because now I have an idea. I'm about to ask her for the kind of favor I would never ask of a stranger. But now that I know where I need to go, I'm willing to try anything to get there. I planted that seed during the board meeting, but in case that doesn't work out—

"Mrs. Scott," I say, "do you live in England? I'm guessing, from your accent—"

"I do, indeed," she says. "You don't remember, but that's where your grandmother and you visited me. In my house in Hyde Park. My poor husband was alive then, bless his soul—"

"Is Hyde Park near London?"

"It's in London," Mrs. Scott says. "Near the center."

I take a breath. "Would it be all right if I visited you some time?"

"I would love it!" she says. "Halli dear, you are always welcome. When would you like to come?"

"Um, soon? I was thinking maybe next week, if that wouldn't be too much trouble. Or maybe I could even fly back with you when you go?"

I know I'm being pushy right now, but I can't let that bother me. Ever since that comm call with Daniel, I've known what I have to do: I have to get to London. The sooner I can talk to him in person, with no one listening, and find out everything he knows about Halli's last hours, the sooner I might be able to solve this whole mess.

"That might be difficult," Mrs. Scott says. "I'm afraid I'm leaving in the morning."

"I could be ready by then," I say. It's easy. I've never even fully unpacked Halli's duffel. The truth is I could be ready five minutes from now.

Mrs. Scott laughs. "Well, dear, since you're so eager, I would love to have your company on the trip home. It's such a long flight. And then you're welcome to stay with me as long as you like."

"Oh, thank you, Mrs. Scott." This time I'm the one to take her hands between mine. "You don't know how much I appreciate it. I promise I won't be any trouble."

"It's a large house for one lonely old woman," Mrs. Scott answers. "I welcome the visit."

"Thank you," I say again. "What time should I be ready in the morning?"

Mrs. Scott looks past my shoulder. "Ah, young . . . Jake, isn't it?" she asks.

"Yes, ma'am," he says. "Kind of you to remember."

I'd been so absorbed in my conversation with Mrs. Scott, I hadn't seen him come up behind us.

"Excuse me," Jake says, "but Halli, can I talk to you for a minute?"

"I'll speak with you later, dear," Mrs. Scott says, squeezing my hand. "Please sit beside me at supper tonight. We'll make our plans then."

"I will," I promise. "Thank you."

Jake waits for her to leave, then asks, "What plans are those?"

I hesitate to tell him, but I don't think I have any choice. He's going to find out soon enough anyway.

"I'm going to stay with her for a little while. Just for a visit."

"I don't think that's a good idea," Jake says.

"What? Why?"

"You need to be careful with her," he tells me.

"Careful with her how?"

"She and your grandmother hated each other. They've been enemies for years."

"Mrs. *Scott*? No way." I turn around and take another look at the sweet little old lady making her rounds about the room. There's no way she hated Ginny—not after all the nice things she said about her. And she wouldn't have been so nice to Ginny's granddaughter if they two of them were enemies. I just don't buy it.

"They must have made up at some point," I tell Jake. "I'm sure they were friends."

"Halli, I'm telling you—the two of them hated each other for years. They had some feud going back decades. I'm sure your grandmother died still hating her."

I just can't believe it.

"That's why I think your parents were surprised," Jake says, "when you aligned yourself with Mrs. Scott, instead of your trustee."

"But—" I'm just about to say I don't know Monsieur Bern, and I don't trust him, when I realize I don't really know where Halli may have stood with him. Maybe she did trust him. Maybe he really was speaking for her. I have no way of knowing.

And the truth is, the same goes for Mrs. Scott. Even though my gut is telling me she's a nice woman with Halli's best interests at heart, maybe my gut is wrong.

"Do you . . . think I made a mistake?" I ask Jake. "In the board meeting?"

He chuckles and shakes his head. "Let's just say you were full of surprises today." Then he grows more serious. "Halli, it's not your head, is it? A memory problem? Because it really was a surprise. From what Monsieur Bern told your parents before the meeting, it sounded like everything had been worked out. Was he wrong? Or did you forget?"

I can't help touching my malaffected head. "I don't know." I'm actually starting to get concerned.

And then some particle of that supposedly injured brain speaks up and reminds me: There's nothing wrong with my head. There never was. That whole story was a lie.

I've never been great at lying. Liars keep their stories straight. Liars remember when they're lying.

"I'm sure I'll be fine," I say. "I just need to sort a few things out."

Jake is still studying me with that worried look on his face. "Halli, I really think you need to see the doctor here—"

"I'm fine. Really. But I need some fresh air."

"I'll come with you," Jake says.

I nearly say yes—it might be good to hear Jake's perspective on that whole board meeting—but what he had to say about Mrs. Scott and Halli's grandmother is really bothering me. And I'm not sure it's actually good for me at this point to find out how badly I might have messed things up for Halli. What's done is done— for now.

If I need to fix things—agree with Monsieur Bern, for example, and let the vote go through the way Halli's parents wanted—I can do that in a month, right? Or better yet, Halli can do it if everyone just leaves me alone for a while and lets me work on the science.

"I think Red and I will just walk by ourselves for a while," I tell him. "I'll see you at dinner tonight—assuming I'm still invited. How mad are H—" I'm about to call them "Halli's parents," but I catch myself. "—my parents?"

Jake shrugs. "I think you can imagine. But no, they're not going to keep you from dinner." He smiles sympathetically. "They might give you the high seas holograph again, though."

Great. Maybe I should have a few of his mother's muffins now, so at least I have something in my stomach. Then not even try to eat dinner at all.

Which reminds me.

"Do you think I can meet your mother?"

Jake seems surprised. "If you want to."

Never mind the walk. Maybe seeing a familiar, friendly face like Elena's—or whatever Will and Lydia's/Jake and Alexa's mother is called here—will be just as nice as some wet air off the beach.

"Do you think she's busy right now?" I ask.

"She's always busy," Jake says. "Now is as good a time as any."

26

The kitchen is enormous. And there are at least ten people in here, scurrying, mixing, sautéing, chopping—whatever it takes to feed a crowd.

One of the workers is Celeste, sitting on a stool, chewing a stalk of celery and stirring a pot on the stove while she talks to her mom.

I wasn't prepared. It's even worse than meeting their father. He was dead, now he's alive. But Elena—Elena has always been alive. And to me she's been like a second mom.

And seeing her, I've never felt so lonely and orphaned in my life.

I wonder if I'm ever going to see my real mother again.

My real life again.

Any of the people, the places, my school, the real Will, the real Lydia, the real Halli—

"Miss Halli!" Celeste cries out. She's just spotted me. Right now I would like nothing better than to run out of here, straight up four flights of stairs, into my room where I can curl up onto my big white bed and cry my miserable eyes out.

"Celeste!" I say back.

And shove every bit of feeling I have to the bottom of my feet where I can stamp on them really hard right now.

Elena turns around. She had her back to me, at the stove, and it's a much stouter back than the Elena's I know, but the stouter her body the better, because I just want to run right to her and bury myself in a hug.

"I'll introduce you," Jake says.

My legs feel like steel beams. I can barely walk. I'm smiling because what else can I do with this face that wants to sob?

"My mother, Olivia," Jake says.

She wipes her hand on her apron before offering it. "Oh, Miss Markham, very nice to meet you. You've been so kind to my girl here. Thank you."

I can't speak. I just smile and nod. And as with her husband Oscar, I'm finding a hard time letting go of her hand.

The real Elena is an excellent cook. My mother and I have counted on her over the years to provide the only real food in our lives. Otherwise the two of us are all cereal and take-out.

It's so strange that the Elena here is a cook, too. Maybe it's part of their DNA.

"Your . . . muffins," I manage to croak out. "So . . . so good."

Olivia smiles shyly. "Thank you so much, Miss Markham. I'm so glad you've enjoyed them."

I nod a little too enthusiastically. I feel like a wooden puppet, with some crazy person working my strings. My limbs don't both work at the same time. My face is frozen in this smile.

Please, Elena, recognize me. Please, somebody, know me.

"I . . . I have to go," I whisper. I turn toward the door, ready to make my escape, but it's too much—it's too precious. I can't just leave like this.

I hug her. Arms around her neck. I hug her and smell her skin and it's not the same. But her face is a face from my life, no matter what the rest of the form is telling me. She has been there for me since I was four. After school, weekends, every time my mom had to go out of town on a trip. Sleepovers, nightmares, vomiting with the flu—it's been her making up a bed for me, reassuring me, wiping my hot face with a cool rag.

Olivia laughs uncertainly, but still she hugs me back. That's all I want. Thank you. Bless you. Help me.

I wipe away a tear. "I should let you get back to

cooking. Sorry to bother you. Hi, Celeste. See you later."

Then I turn around and run. There's nothing else to do. My heart is already cracking in a thousand different places and if I don't run to keep ahead of it, it's going to shatter all over this room.

I miss my life.

I miss my mother.

I miss everyone and everything.

Please let this nightmare end.

Help me fix it.

Help me go home.

27

I am running on the beach in my cowgirl outfit, the sun is nearly down, and all I want is a good cleansing cry, but Jake has almost caught up with me.

Red is in the water again, so at least he's happy. He comes bounding out as soon as he sees Jake, hoping for a stick.

"Not tonight," Jake tells him. "Sorry, buddy."

The dog shakes the water off, and lopes along beside us.

I slow to a walk. We don't speak, Jake and I, and I appreciate that. He walks parallel to me, and reaches down to take my hand.

I appreciate that, too.

We walk for maybe ten minutes that way, Jake's warm hand intertwined with mine. I know I shouldn't encourage him, but right now I can't seem to care about any of that. All I want is the comfort and the contact. So I don't pull away or try to stop it.

The sun in this part of the world doesn't just fade, it blips. One moment it's a yellow lump on the horizon, the next it just disappears into the sea.

In the dark I don't mind telling him what's on my mind.

"I'm sorry about all that. I'm just homesick. I didn't really know how much. It just hit me all of a sudden."

"My parents seem to affect you," Jake says.

I laugh, despite myself. "Yeah. Well. I don't know."

My teeth are chattering again. I never seem to know how to dress myself here. Halli's sweater is still sitting up in the closet, inside her duffel, when I'd really love to be wearing it now.

Jake notices the shivering.

"Halli. Wait."

He lets go of my hand so he can take his jacket off.

"No," I say, "you don't have to—"

But it's already on me. This time he makes sure I slip my arms into the sleeves.

Then Jake reaches back and frees my hair from its ponytail. He spreads my hair across my shoulders, and even tucks some of it forward, into the collar, shielding my neck from the cold.

"Better?" he asks.

My voice is just a whisper. "Why are you so nice to me?"

"You still don't understand, do you?"

"Understand what?"

"I love you, Halli. I'd do anything for you. You should know that by now."

He wraps me in his arms. And this time I'm the one who starts it. I kiss him like I never kissed Daniel, like I always thought I might kiss Will, I kiss him like I wanted to last night, before light shined in my eyes and I came back to my senses.

I don't want to come to my senses. Not now. Not for this minute. I want to empty my head of every thought, every fear, every worry, every plan. I just want to feel, for once, feel someone holding me like this, his strong arms around me, his mouth on mine, his fingers tangled in my long thick hair, tugging it back to tilt my face up to his, his body so close against mine I can feel his pulse, his warmth through our clothes, I can forget where I am or who I am or what I have to do. It's just me. Him. The beginnings of a cold, starless night. I have nowhere to be, nothing else to do but stand here for all eternity, kissing until my mind is a blank.

28

It's eight-thirty, and Mrs. Scott still hasn't arrived at dinner.

The theme in here tonight is a tropical motif, which seems strange since we're on such a different kind of island. But there are palm trees swaying, white sandy beach, coconuts falling from the ceiling here and there and cracking at our feet. A toucan with his oversized beak swoops over the table every now and then, and yep—here comes the rain. It's been raining on and off every five minutes or so, sparkly lighting effects with none of the wet. Very disorienting, as usual. Although this time Red is sleeping through it.

I'm seated next to one of the other ladies who was at the board meeting, and even though she and I smile at each other any time we accidentally make eye contact, she's not one for much conversation—with me or the person on her other side. She just sits there sniffing the food, tasting little bits, sniffing the next bit, working her way around the plate. Maybe she's like one of those poison tasters from the old days. Maybe Halli's parents are paranoid.

They haven't said one word to me—either of them. I caught Halli's mother looking my way when I first walked in, but after she frowned at my lack of fancy— just a clean pair of Halli's jeans, and that sweater I wish I'd worn earlier—she turned away and never looked at me again.

But Jake has looked. Several times. And given me that secret smile of his. It makes my cheeks feel as warm as if we really were dining beneath a brilliant tropical sun. And it makes me wish we were outside again, alone, now that I'm dressed properly, instead of in here among a whole crowd of people I don't care anything about.

The only person I was interested in seeing at dinner tonight was Mrs. Scott, but now it doesn't look like that's going to happen. She isn't the only one who's missing: that man she called Jeffrey is gone, too. I remember him saying he wanted to go back tonight. Is it possible Mrs. Scott went with him? But then why didn't she send me a message of some sort? Why did she leave without me?

Maybe Jake really was right about her. Maybe

everything nice thing she said to me was a lie. Maybe she was setting me up for disappointment in some sick plan to get back at Ginny Markham.

But I just don't believe it. Sometimes you think you know a person, sometimes you don't. And I just feel in my heart that the Mrs. Scott I met and spoke to—the one who was so kind to Halli—was the real deal. I can't imagine she was secretly harboring some evil plot to hurt me.

But now I don't know what I'm going to do about getting myself to England.

I suppose I can ask Halli's parents for the use of their plane. I don't know how committed they feel to looking good in front of this group. Maybe if I ask them tonight at dinner, in front of everyone, they'll have to say yes. I'll tell them I'm ready to start visiting some of the company's locations, starting with London next week.

As if reading my mind, the man on my right says, "Will you be coming to Sydney, Miss Markham?"

"Oh. Yeah. Um, probably. I'm not sure yet."

"We would welcome the interest." The man holds out his hand. "Anthony Pruitt. Knew your grandmother. Wonderful, fiery woman."

I shake his hand. "Yes, sir. Thank you. She was."

Mr. Pruitt lowers his voice. "Voted for you today. By all means, take your month. Would have given you the four months. Don't agree with this whole scheme."

He sits back up straight and clears his throat. "How are you finding the weather here?"

I notice what Mr. Pruitt has just noticed: that that history reporter, Bryan, is currently pointing his over-sized square binoculars directly at us.

"Oh, it's nice," I say. "Kind of cold and wet, but . . . you know. Nice."

Bryan has now moved on to filming other people. Mr. Pruitt drops his chin and speaks again in a low voice.

"Don't ever sell your shares," he tells me. "You hang on to those, just like your grandmother did. There's a big future coming—"

"If I can have your attention," Halli's father says. He's standing, commanding the room as usual with his authoritative voice. "Thank you for your time and attendance here this weekend. I'm sorry you all had to come such a long way for nothing—"

He looks pointedly at me. How subtle.

"—but I look forward to completing this matter one month from now. As you might imagine, there's always more work to be done, so I'll have to leave you now, but you're welcome to stay for dessert. I know some of you are leaving in the morning, so I'll say my goodbye now."

I've started to tune him out, assuming anything else he has to say is just a formality for the board people, but suddenly he says my name:

"Halli?"

The conversations all around the table seem to die at the same time. I look up, probably too wide-eyed to pull off not looking panicked.

I can't even open my mouth. I just go with, "Hm?"

"Your mother and I need to speak with you. If you would come with us now."

I've never liked getting in trouble, and I have the feeling that's what this is. It was too much to hope that he'd just let me get away with my whole rebellion this afternoon. In the flurry of other activity, I forgot that at some point I was going to have to answer to Halli's parents, and that they weren't going to be happy with me at all.

I slide back my chair, and slowly get up from the table. If this were a movie, I'd hear some funeral march in the distance.

"Come on, Red," I whisper. When a girl is about to be punished, she likes to have her faithful companion at her side.

I leave behind the tropical jungle, and follow Halli's parents to my fate.

29

"Bryan?" Halli's father calls to the reporter at the last minute. "If you would accompany us as well."

I don't know whether to be relieved or suspicious. I decide to go with relieved. Although I really wish he had asked Jake to come instead.

The four of us leave the dining hall and walk out to the base of the Grand Staircase.

Halli's father motions toward the reporter. "Mr. Stewart here has made a request."

"Seems like you're off on a new odyssey, Miss Markham," Bryan says. "I talked to my producer, and we'd like the exclusive on it. If you're willing."

"The exclusive . . . what?" I ask.

"Story," he says. "They want to send me along. Fly-on-the-wall type of thing. I promise I won't be intrusive. You'll forget I'm there."

"I'm sorry, I don't . . . understand."

Halli's mother sighs with impatience. "They want to film you. Touring our facilities. Remember? Isn't that why you asked for your month? Isn't that what your whole outburst was all about?"

"Yes. Right. Great."

My brain is working at full capacity, trying to think this through.

Because in one way, it's exactly what I want—better than I could have hoped for. To have some official reason for going exactly where I want to go, all the details arranged. I'm sure Halli's parents will send me in their plane, put me up at some hotel, make sure I'm taken care of—

But on the other hand, it's exactly what I don't need: some nosy reporter tagging along, keeping track of everything I do.

And then that makes me think of the tracking: Halli's parents will know where I'm going all the time anyway. It's not like I can just fly to England and then disappear. So I might as well just accept that, and take what help I can get along the way.

"Okay," I say, "sure. That sounds great. In fact, I was hoping to leave immediately—like maybe tomorrow, if we can."

I'm looking at Bryan for permission, when really it's

Halli's parents who get to decide.

"And go where?" Halli's mother asks. She sounds very put-upon. Like the effort of even having to talk to me is too much.

"I'd like to start in London," I say.

"Fine," Halli's mother says. "Alexa, call Transport. Let them know."

"Yes, ma'am."

I didn't even know she was there, standing outside the doorway to the dining hall.

And she isn't alone.

"I'd like to go with her," Jake says, coming over to join us. "If you can spare me, Dr. Bellows. I think it would be good for Miss Markham to have an escort. Someone who can show her around the facility, make sure she talks to the right people—"

My pulse has just jolted into a sprint. What is Jake doing?

Halli's mother and father look at each other. Then Halli's mother gives a subtle nod.

"Keep it short," Halli's father says. "No more than a week."

"A week should be enough," Jake says, "don't you think, Miss Markham?"

"Um . . . yeah. I do. A week."

But I'm still trying to process the offer. Do I want Jake there with me, or not?

Not. For several good reasons, including the fact that

I'll feel guilty enough around Daniel without the other guilty party present. And then there's the fact that the reason I'm going is to find out what happened to the girl who really belongs in this body—

But Halli's parents are already working out the details with Jake, and Bryan is off on a comm call to his producer, and I'm just standing here trying to sort out everything that's happening. Is it a good thing, or a bad? Aren't I getting what I want?

"Be careful what you say and do," Halli's mother warns me. "Remember, you're representing us and the company now, not only yourself. Jake, you'll watch her?"

"Every minute," he says.

I meet his eyes, then look away.

I think I'm in trouble.

In more ways than one.

30

I am sitting on a plane.

A private jet.

A much larger one, because we are flying farther.

There is a dog at my feet. I love that dog.

There is a guy sitting across from me, a guy who looks like the one I've been in love with all my life, and yet a guy I met just two days ago and might be falling in love with again.

"You think I'm going to let you go alone?" he told me in private last night, after all the details had been worked out. We took Red out for one last walk before bedtime, and talked about everything that had gone on.

"I'm worried about you," Jake said. "You need to see a doctor. I'm not letting you out of my sight until you do." He kissed my neck. "And even after that."

I know it's wrong, and it's stupid, and it's not going to end anywhere close to happily, but I can't seem to help myself right now. There's so much else in my life that feels uncertain and out of control, and even though this situation with Jake is obviously both of those things, too, at least it makes me feel good for a while, and lets me forget everything else for that brief space of time when he's holding me and kissing me and telling me all of the things I've always wanted to be told.

Whether he calls me by the right name or not.

"Miss Markham," Bryan calls from the back of the plane. "My producer would like a few words with you."

I exchange a look with Jake, then take a deep breath. Time to go lie some more.

There's a woman's head hovering above Bryan's tablet.

Bryan introduces us. "My producer, Faith Newsom."

She has a nice face, here in 3-D, short reddish-blond hair, large blue eyes, and a warm, genuine smile.

"Thanks for agreeing to this," she tells me. "I know you haven't wanted any publicity since . . . well, for a while. We're honored you chose History 6 for your first exclusive interview."

"Oh," I say, "sure. Of course." Even though it wasn't my choice, it was Halli's parents'.

"I don't know if you remember," Ms. Newsom says, "but we were part of the team who met you at the end of your row across the Atlantic with your grandmother."

I smile at that. Even though I've never seen the footage, I've heard about it, and I still think the whole thing sounds so amazing. I think Halli was only twelve at the time. Wow.

"I'm sorry," I say, "I don't remember. It was all . . . kind of a blur."

"I'm not surprised," Ms. Newsom says. "Sharks, dehydration, third-degree sunburn, your grandmother's broken collar bone—"

"Yeah," I say, "good times."

Bryan and his producer both laugh.

"You're in good hands," Ms. Newsom says. "Bryan is one of our best. He won't get in your way. He's just going to shadow you while you're in London, be the viewers' eyes and ears. People are very curious about what you're doing these days, as I'm sure you can imagine."

"Yeah," I say. "I guess I can."

"Well, if there's anything at all you need from us," she says, "feel free to ask Bryan or to contact me. All right?"

"Yes, ma'am. Thank you."

"Please," she says. "Faith."

"Then Halli," I tell her back.

"Thanks, Halli," she says. "We'll be talking again soon."

The holographic head disappears. Bryan puts away his tablet.

I watch it go back into his bag. *"If there's anything at all you need from us, feel free to ask Bryan."* Maybe that's what I'm going to have to do.

Because even though I brought the loaner tablet with me from the island, it's not like that's going to do me any good. I still haven't figured out how to work it, or how to access that search function Celeste used to find Daniel, and even if I could accomplish both things, there's still the problem of Halli's parents' snooping and listening in to whatever I do. So I might as well have packed a piece of driftwood from the shore, for all the good that particular item of technology is going to do me.

So maybe Bryan is the answer, although I'm going to have to ask him the right way. He is a reporter, after all, and I can't have him wondering why Halli Markham might be interested in finding a certain young gentleman in London.

Or have Jake overhear me asking and wonder that, too.

I'm just going to have to figure it out as I go, just like I seem to be doing with every other aspect of my life right now.

Back home Lydia is always trying to get me to be more "yoga" by "going with the flow" and "not pushing the river," and all sorts of other catchy phrases. But pushing the river has always felt better to me. I like to get in there and make things happen, not just sit back and take it all as it comes.

Which is why I'm stuck here in a parallel universe in a parallel body.

So maybe I need to shake up my tactics a little.

What would Lydia do right now? How would she be all yoga? She'd lean back in her seat, take a nice calming breath, and just be here in the moment.

And right at this moment I'm sitting across from a reporter who apparently is going to be with me night and day for the next week. So I might as well get used to it.

"So," I say to him, "that Faith woman seems nice. How long have you worked for her?"

"About five years," he says. "That job with you and your grandmother was my first. I probably wasn't that much older than you are now."

"So you just . . . go wherever she says and film whatever's interesting?" I still don't really understand why he was at that board meeting. Did Halli's parents invite him, or did his producer send him?

"I bounce around all of the organizations," he says. "Whoever has the next job. We all do that. Way to make a living."

"Oh. Uh-huh. I see." I've run out of things to say.

"That Faith, though," Bryan says. "She's really top

rate. I've worked for a lot of history producers over the years, and some of them can be real—"

"Excuse me?" I interrupt, suddenly sitting up straight. "What did you just call her?"

"No, not her," Bryan says. "I'm saying some of the other ones can be real—"

"No, no—before that. Faith is a history producer? That's what you call her?"

"Yes," he says. "Why?"

Why? *Why?* Because right here, right in front of me might be the unveiling of a certified miracle.

"So you know other history producers?" I ask.

"Sure. A lot of them," Bryan says. "Why?"

I'm trying really hard to stay calm, and not let Bryan know that his answer to my next question might be the most important answer he's ever given someone in his life.

Because I have heard the term "history producer" only once before in my life, and it made such a little impression on me at the time, I'm surprised I even remember it.

It was when Daniel was showing me some biographical information about himself—a list of his awards, some details about his family and his schooling —and there among the details were his parents' names and their professions.

His mother, an archaeologist.

His father, a history producer. I had no idea what that meant at the time—nor did I think I'd ever care.

And I didn't pay attention to their names, because why should I care about those, either? And the problem is all the people here seem to take their mothers' last names, so knowing Daniel's last name is Everett doesn't help me identify his father.

"There was this one producer," I say, choosing my words carefully. "I met him at one of my things a few years ago, and I can't remember his name, but I think he said his wife was an archaeologist, and I just thought that was really interesting. Do you know who I'm talking about?"

"Oh, sure," Bryan says. "Sam Wheeler. Great guy. Worked for him on a few productions myself."

I'm sitting perfectly still. I want to jump up and down in my seat. I blink a few times just to expend the energy.

"Do you . . ." I calmly clear my throat. "You wouldn't happen to know where I could find him?"

I'm sure Jake is listening right now—his seat isn't that far from us. But I can't turn around to check, because I don't want him to see me do that and think that this is important.

"Sam works for History 14," Bryan says. "Right there in London, matter of fact."

"Hm." I nod like it's no big deal. "Okay, thanks."

Then I excuse myself and go back to my original seat. And give Jake a casual little smile.

"Everything all right?" he asks.

"Yep. Just fine."

I look out the window to pretend I'm not excited out of my mind right now.

"Who's that guy you were talking about?" Jake asks.

"This girl's father," I say, which is at least partially true. Sam Wheeler does have two children, a girl and a boy. "I was thinking I might try to look her up while I'm over there. I think she lives in London."

"What's her name?" Jake asks.

"Sarah. Sarah Everett. Really nice girl."

Jake leans forward in his seat. He looks past me to make sure we're not being watched, or worse, filmed.

Then he whispers, "You're a really nice girl. Wish we were alone right now."

I nod and give him a smile. Jake leans back again like there's nothing going on.

I force myself to look out the window.

If this is what it's like to go with the flow—to stop pushing the river—then maybe I've been doing it wrong all along. Maybe I should just wait for things to drop right into my lap. Because this piece of news might be the best thing I've heard in the past forty-eight hours.

I have a way to find Daniel. Which is fantastic.

Even if there's a whole complicated river after that.

31

It's late here in London, some time close to midnight. The city is beautiful and busy, and it's traveling in the wrong direction. I've almost been hit by cars three times in a row now. Jake keeps having to pull me back on the curb.

"Look right, then left, then right again," he advises. "The opposite of what you're used to."

I have to say it out loud to myself while I do it, just to make sure. "Right, left, right." We make it safely across the street. Into the next danger zone.

Halli's parents own an apartment. A "flat," they call it here. Jake says it has two bedrooms. There are three of us.

Obviously Jake and Bryan will have to share a room, but still. It's the proximity thing. I've never spent the night somewhere so close to someone I could potentially be making out with 24/7.

We enter the high-rise, and are greeted by a man in a very snappy uniform. I thought Lyman dressed well. This man, decked out in bright red and gold, looks like he could be leading a parade.

"Miss Markham!" he says with a huge smile. "Welcome. Your parents let us know you were coming. So good to have you here, Miss."

"Thank you."

"Bates, how are you?" Jake asks.

"Very well, sir, thank you."

"This is Bryan Stewart," Jake says. "He'll be staying with us for a few days."

Bates gives a little bow. "Good to meet you, sir."

"Is the flat ready?" Jake says.

"Checked it myself," Bates says. "Everything for the lady."

All the way up the elevator, I'm wondering what that means. As soon as Jake opens the door to the flat, I see.

There are roses *everywhere*. White ones, red ones, pink, yellow, lavender. The whole place smells like perfume and bubble bath. I'm actually kind of embarrassed the guys have to stay here, too.

There are fruit bowls piled high with grapes, oranges, apples, pears. A platter covered with crackers and spreads. A basket full of cookies. Several plates holding a variety of sandwiches. And three bottles of champagne.

I wander into the next room. There's a bedroom in there, so girly it almost makes my head hurt. Curtains and bedspread and tablecloths and lampshades, all made out of the same flowery cloth—white fabric dotted with pink and red roses. It's a miniature flower explosion.

Red doesn't seem to mind. He hops onto the pile of pillows on the bed and settles right in.

On a hunch, I open the closet. Just like the one in the mansion, it's stuffed full of dresses, gowns, all sorts of frilly outfits. And once again there are more shoes in my size than I'd ever wear in a year.

And once again I throw Halli's battered duffel onto the perfect bedspread. And have a little smile to myself, knowing I'm once more going to rebel and wear what Halli would wear—what I want to wear.

Jake stands in the doorway behind me. "What do you think?"

"Hold on, let me check the bathroom."

I walk into the little space off of the bedroom, and find a claw-foot tub, currently filled with two huge bouquets of roses. I think I sense a theme here. I'm surprised there are no roses floating in the toilet.

I look at Jake and have to laugh. "Who does this?"

"Their decorator," he says. "I forgot which one. Each property is different."

"If you guys want to send all these flowers away, I'll understand."

"Why?" Jake says. "They're for you. Enjoy them."

We walk back out to the front room, where Bryan is sitting in one of the frilly chairs, basically stuffing his face. I noticed he also sampled freely all the food they kept offering him on the airplane. Reporters must not get to eat like that too often.

"So," Bryan says, not bothering to swallow his food first. "I assume we start first thing in the morning?"

"Right after breakfast," Jake answers. "If that's all right with you, Miss Markham."

"Hm. Sure." I'm not really paying attention, because I'm busy looking around the room, trying to figure out where these guys are supposed to sleep. There's only one couch, and it doesn't look like it opens out into a bed. Considering how rich Halli's parents' are, I can't imagine they expect people to roll a cot in here or sleep on the floor.

Jake is now gathering up some food for himself. "So when you're ready," he tells me, "just knock on the door."

"What door?" I ask.

He stuffs a cookie into his mouth and points. There's a painted white door stuck in the middle of the wall. I go over and open it.

And here's the rest of the flat. I thought the rooms

we were in were much too tiny for Halli's parents' taste. Now I see what I was missing.

This other side is about twice as large as my side. There's a huge living room, a decent-sized kitchen, a bedroom with two king-sized beds in it. I think the one on my side is only a double.

The colors in here are completely subdued—just tan walls, tan rugs, boring, although I'm sure expensive, antiques. And no flowers or fruit bowls or champagne. No wonder Jake and Bryan are loading up.

Bryan has half a sandwich in his mouth, and another whole one on his plate. He's also carrying one of the bottles of champagne. "Hope you don't mind. I heard you don't drink."

Why does he know that, and Halli's parents don't?

"No, of course not," I say. "Help yourself."

He reaches back for one last cookie. I hand him the whole basket, which he wedges under his arm. "See you in the morning."

"Yeah, see you," I say.

"I'll be right in," Jake tells him. "I just need to go over a few things with Miss Markham about tomorrow's agenda." Then he closes the door. And quietly locks it.

Then so fast I can barely react, he pulls me to one of the walls Bryan isn't on the other side of, flattens me against it, and starts kissing the living wits out of me.

"I've been waiting for this all day," Jake whispers, and I realize I have been, too.

I used to pride myself on having a brain that works. I liked challenging it with the hardest physics books I could find, with the longest hours I could spend studying, with the highest ambition for myself about which college I might get into.

But lately I seem to take a lot more satisfaction in finding the things that allow me not to think at all—that grueling workout with Ferguson yesterday, and these workouts with Jake, which are sometimes just as sweaty, but involve much less exertion. I can understand now how making out got to be so popular. Right now I can't think of anything more rewarding to do with my time.

When we finally come up for air, Jake grins at me. Then he rests his forehead against mine, and whispers, "I should probably get back in there. We don't want him wondering."

And I'm suddenly very grateful for there being a history reporter in the next room. Because right now he might be the only thing standing between me and making the wrong choice—a choice I might regret later, once I get all my brain cells working again.

"Yeah. Okay. You should. In a minute." And this time I flip him around and press him against the wall.

Which I'm somehow sure is a thing Halli would do.

Finally we both have to breathe again. Jake smoothes my hair away from my face. It's the perfect time to look into his eyes. Those dark, familiar eyes I've grown up knowing, and always wished would look at me this way.

But for the first time, I realize something: I'm glad he's not Will. Will would never do this. He would never hold me like this, kiss me this way, say the things Jake says to me. Will is my friend. He could never be anything more. It would feel weird if he ever was.

I think I finally just got that. Which is kind of amazing to me.

"I should go," Jake says again.

"You should," I agree. "Right away." Then I close my eyes because he's kissing me again.

Sometimes it's best not to think.

Sometimes it's the only thing you can do.

32

Halli's parents must own half the world. At least that's the impression they must be trying to give when you first walk into one of their buildings.

Everything is all marble and gold and dark, shiny wood, and there's no point in putting up a wall anywhere if you can put up floor-to-ceiling windows instead. So if you walk in at the right time, like we just did, the sun coming in through the lobby can blind you and make you a little dizzy.

"Miss Markham?"

There's a man holding out his hand for me to shake. I shield my eyes with one hand, and offer him my other.

"Jake," he says, "good to see you again."

"You too, sir." Jake introduces us. "This is Johnson Chilton, Chief Operating Officer of the London office."

Bryan is off to the side, filming.

"Where would you like to start today, Miss Markham?" Mr. Chilton asks. "Operations, accounting, off-site facilities, research and development—"

"Research," I say. "That sounds good." Give me some science. That, maybe, I can handle.

I didn't sleep well last night. Maybe it was the gagging perfume of those flowers, or the gnawing emptiness in my stomach once I realized I hadn't eaten since the morning, or maybe it was the jet lag or the time difference.

Or maybe it was the guy sleeping on the other side of a door I purposely made myself lock.

I always thought "tossed and turned" was just a quaint cliché, but I can confirm that a person in my position last night actually does toss and turn. So much so that if Halli's parents were watching my tracking information, they must have wondered whether the microchip in my chest had gone haywire. Nobody can twist and flip and flop around in a bed that many times in one night. But she can if her mind has suddenly turned back on and decided to process things for the next seven or eight hours.

Things like:

Why did Mrs. Scott leave? Is she back here in London? Can I find her and talk to her? I don't care what Jake says—I know Mrs. Scott is on my side. And I believe she can help me figure out how to protect Halli's interests in her parents' company.

But why should I care? I'm just a temporary tenant in this body. If I can find Halli, if I can reverse what I've done, then isn't it Halli's choice how she wants to handle things with her parents?

Jake said Halli already spoke with Monsieur Bern and agreed with him how things should be handled. Why is it up to me to mess with that? Why don't I just butt out?

But if Halli didn't know—if she was going to find out new information at that board meeting, just like I did—then wasn't it the right thing to try to delay that vote, and buy Halli some more time?

And what if—this was my worst episode of tossing and turning, by far—what if I'm wrong? What if I can't undo it? What if Halli is lost or dead, or if I just can't undo this whole thing? Then what?

Then it's me. Me here. Only me. And this is my own future I'm working toward.

I had to get out of bed on that one. Pace around the room. But then I was afraid Jake might hear my footsteps and think I was up, and he might think I was hoping he was up, too—

So I made myself go back to bed.

And that's when I thought, *please*. This can't be how I spend the rest of my life. I'm not saying it's awful—I mean, Halli obviously leads a very privileged life—but it's not the life I want.

It's been too long since I thought about what I, Audie Masters, actually want. I mean aside from getting out of this mess. My real life seems so far in the past now, it's hard to remember what I used to care about.

My mom, obviously. My friends Lydia and Will. Getting Will to love me. Those are some of the daily basics right there.

But I also cared a LOT about getting into college. Columbia University, specifically. It's why I'm here now, in this universe—because I just had to keep trying to come up with something that would outshine my grades and convince Columbia they should let me in.

And now, it just seems so insignificant. Completely irrelevant. I know I used to obsess over it, worry about it night and day, but now I just can't seem to care.

It must be like that for anyone who has to face a genuine crisis in his or her life. You have this list in your head of all the things you think are important, then BOOM, some tragedy or shock comes into your life, and suddenly all you care about is surviving and being with the people you love.

Which then led me to this: who is there to love over here? Halli isn't here, so she's out. Halli's parents are horrid, so they're out. I suppose I could create a new circle of friends out of the few people I met on that island and actually liked: Ferguson, Celeste, Jake. Jake's parents, Oscar and Olivia. Maybe I could run away with Jake's family. Convince them to leave Alexa behind, and ask them to come set up a new household with me.

Is there anyone else? Not really. That's a pretty pathetic number. Then again, is it any different in my own, real life? There's just my mom, occasionally my dad, Lydia, Will, and their mom Elena. That's it. Either way, my circle of love is intimately small.

So we're really just talking about a trade. Five people for five people. Halli would have made it six.

As the night wore on, I realized there were a few more people to add to the equation: Professor Whitfield on one side, Daniel and Sarah on the other.

And me. I was one of the people. One of the people I'm missing over here.

I haven't really thought much about that. I've felt sorry for myself because I miss my mom and my familiar life, but I haven't really noticed I miss *me*.

It gets tiring to be someone else. I have moments where I feel like I'm doing an okay job pretending to be Halli, but I'd much rather do an expert job at being myself. I remember one night when I was talking to Daniel—that night when he showed me his own biography—and I said I felt so underachieving and inadequate compared to Halli.

And what did Daniel say? That he liked me better.

Yes, Halli had done all these exciting things with her life, but he wanted to be with me, not her.

And then my stomach really started hurting. Because what kind of a person am I? A guy says something like that to you, and you forget about him and start making out with the next guy who comes along?

Granted, Jake is . . . irresistible, if I have to be honest, but a good person—a strong person—would resist.

Especially when that person knows very well that Jake is not in love with *her*.

And by then, the sun was already starting to come up, and I don't think I'd accidentally fallen asleep at all.

Which is why I'm now finding it so hard to concentrate while Mr. Chilton explains to me all the wonderful things they do at this fabulous London facility.

"Are you familiar at all with photosynthesis, Miss Markham?"

"What? Oh. Yeah." I blink myself awake. "Photosynthesis."

Biology was never my favorite subject. I was tense all year, thinking we might have to dissect something.

"We consider this a type of replicated photosynthesis," Mr. Chilton says. "Using sunlight and your parents' hydro-catalytic process to split water molecules and generate hydrogen."

He smiles to himself. "Sorry—probably more technical than you're interested in. My wife is always telling me to speak English. Let's just say your parents have discovered a way to use the same amount of water in that cup of coffee you're holding to provide enough power for this entire building for a day, or to fuel that jet you flew over on last night."

Now I'm a little more awake. I was curious about that movie Halli's parents showed at the beginning of the board meeting, but then I never got to find out more—so much else happened after that. But now here's my chance.

"How does it work?" I ask Mr. Chilton. "I really don't understand."

"The chemistry is fairly advanced," he says. "I'm not sure you'd be interested in all the details. I could show you a film that provides an overview—"

"I think I've already seen it," I say. "And really, I would be interested in all the details. If you don't mind."

Mr. Chilton and Jake exchange a look. Jake shrugs.

"I'm afraid . . ." Mr. Chilton looks over at Bryan, who's been filming us this whole time. "You see, it's proprietary information, Miss Markham. Top secret, if you will. Only certain people . . ."

Bryan lowers his binoculars. "Don't worry," he says. "I'll wait outside. I have to return a few calls anyway."

He's just about to step out alone when I have an idea.

"I just want to make sure he's . . . you know, okay about the whole thing." Without waiting for Jake or Mr. Chilton to answer, I quickly follow Bryan out of the room.

"Can you do me a favor?" I ask him. I turn around to make sure Jake didn't follow me out. "I was wondering . . . could you maybe contact that producer we were talking about yesterday? Sam Wheeler."

"Sure," Bryan says. "You want to talk to him?"

"No, no—I won't have time. But if you could . . . maybe give him a message? Tell him where we are today, and see if maybe his children might want to meet us later for dinner or something."

"His children?"

"Yeah. They're my age. I kind of know them a little. It would be fun to see them. I think you'd like them."

I wonder if Bryan can hear the tension in my voice or see the sweat starting to bead up on my lip. I smile and try to seem normal.

"Sounds good," Bryan says. "If you don't mind me asking them some questions—broadening out the interview."

"Oh. Okay. I guess." I'm not sure what else to say. It seems like a fair request, coming from a reporter— especially considering that's the whole reason he's here with me.

"Miss Markham?" Jake asks from the doorway.

"Right. Coming." I turn back to Bryan. "Nothing big," I say. "Just if they're not busy or anything."

Then I run back into the room to learn some chemistry.

Knowing I've just set into motion a whole chain reaction of my own.

33

"Halli Markham!" Sarah's voice rings out over the lobby, hours sooner than I expected it, but some assistant came and found me and now I've just walked through the door on the far side of the building, out onto the marble floor, afternoon sunlight streaming in through the windows, and I can't believe how completely relieved and overjoyed I am to hear Sarah's voice and see her blonde hair in the distance and see the guy walking next to her until she takes off at a run and leaves him behind so she can throw herself at me and hug me so hard it's a good thing Halli is so strong or her bones would have cracked.

Sarah is breathless. "You're monstrous! You unforgivable sneak! Why didn't you tell us you were coming?"

I look past her to the smile on Daniel's face. Obviously he never told her about our conversation the other night. Either he wanted to surprise her if I did come, or not disappoint her if I didn't.

"And Red!" Sarah says, letting go of me and crouching down to shower the dog with love. "How are you, you handsome boy?" Red's tail couldn't wag any harder.

I watch Daniel as he walks the rest of the way. He's still limping slightly from that ankle sprain in the Alps, but the rest of him looks as good as it ever did. He's wearing dark pants and a charcoal sweater that looks really nice with his light hair, and he's shaved since the last time I saw him in the mountains.

He has a nice face. Open and honest, with warm brown eyes that really look at you when you're talking, and this kind of smart-aleck smile that lets you know he's on to you when you're lying, like I tried to do when we first met and I claimed to be Halli's cousin. Not only did Daniel see through that, but he had facts to back himself up. He busted me as soon as we were alone, but he was nice about it.

And then I had to accidentally vanish right in front of his eyes and almost give the poor guy a heart attack.

But he took it. He's smart and he's quick, and he could understand the science once I explained it to him, and no matter how many weird things kept happening, he always took it. I could count on him to be calm and rational. Which I think is why I always felt safe around him. I never really thought about that before, but now I do. Because I feel safe right now, just seeing him again.

Which is why I know I can't stick to my original plan. I was going to wait until we were alone. Tell him gently, gradually. Give him time for it to sink in.

But forget it. I can't. He's just going to have to take it.

So I close the distance between us, don't wait for him to get all the way, hurry to him and hug him—harder than he was ready for, because I'm Halli, after all, and he and Halli are just friends—and I keep holding on as I bring my mouth up to his ear and whisper, "It's me. Audie. Don't say anything. It's me in here. Halli's missing. I'll tell you everything later."

He pulls away and holds me at arm's length and gazes into my face. Looks at me hard in the eyes. I look back at him as deeply as I can so maybe he can see it's me in here, and I nod.

He isn't smiling anymore. Not one little bit.

But now the others are around us: Sarah, Jake, Bryan filming it all. Mr. Chilton, waiting patiently to see if I need anything more from our visit here today, or if I'll be leaving.

Which I think he'd like very much to happen, considering how our last few hours together have gone. He was expecting a young woman with no background or interest in science. But he got me instead. I might prefer physics, but I've still had three years of advanced chemistry, and that causes a person to ask a lot of questions when she's shown the kind of technology Halli's parents' have invented. Questions Mr. Chilton wasn't always comfortable answering.

"You're staying with us," Sarah tells me. "You know that, don't you? You're sleeping in my tiny bedroom in our parents' unreasonably tiny house, and I don't care if you have to leave the most luxurious, colossal lodgings to do it. I will not be ashamed, I will not be deterred. I refuse to let you out of my sight. Do you understand me?"

"Who could ever argue with you?" I smile. And it feels like a relief. Because it's almost like I'm home. Like I'm back amongst my people. Even though Daniel still looks seriously shocked, I feel better than I have in days.

"And these gorgeous men are . . . ?" Sarah asks.

I introduce her to Mr. Chilton, Jake, and Bryan. And if I'm not mistaken, Bryan has already taken a special interest. He's put down his camera binoculars now and is looking at Sarah with his bare eyes. And he seems pretty happy with the view.

I steal a look at Daniel. He still hasn't said one word. He's watching me, though, no doubt trying to see for himself that what I said is true.

"No Audie?" Sarah asks me.

"Uh, no," I answer quickly, "she couldn't make it this time. Everyone, this is Daniel, Sarah's brother."

He gives them all a silent nod.

Now I'm really getting worried. I shouldn't have told him that way. He's not going to be able to just act naturally about it, the way I've had to do. I should have waited. That was stupid of me.

"I'm certain what you're doing here is very important," Sarah tells me, "but I'm afraid you'll have to leave with us now. Daniel and I have made certain preparations, and you're wanted elsewhere."

She turns to Mr. Chilton. "Sir, I know you must think me the most impertinent girl, but these are very special circumstances, and I'm afraid I can't explain more. So please forgive us, but we must steal this person from your presence."

"Miss . . . Markham?" Mr. Chilton asks me.

"It's fine," I tell him. "I'm going to think about what you showed me, and if I have any more questions, Jake can bring me back. Thank you for your time, Mr. Chilton. I really appreciate it."

He gives me a slight bow, then shakes Jake's hand and takes off at a rapid pace like he wants to disappear behind a door before I can change my mind.

"It's all arranged," Sarah says. "You'll have to come with us now. Your friends are welcome to join us, of course."

I wish she hadn't said that. But I guess it's natural, and polite.

"It's . . . probably going to be boring for you," I tell Jake. "We'll just be catching up, talking about people you don't know—"

"No, I want to come," Jake says, smiling at me.

"I'd like to come, too," Bryan says, his gaze still glued to Sarah.

"Done!" she says. "Off with us. Daniel and I took transit, so if you have a private car at your disposal, we wouldn't dream of snubbing it. Would we, Dan?"

"Halli?" he says. "May I speak with you?"

"Um . . . sure. Why don't you go get the car?" I say to Jake. "We'll meet you outside."

He looks from Daniel to me. "I'm sure the car is there. We can all go out together."

"Halli?" Daniel repeats.

"Sure. Here. I'll be right back."

I walk with Daniel as far away as I dare without making Jake think there's something going on. He probably already thinks it. When I glance back, he's watching.

"We can't talk about it here," I whisper.

"It's really you."

"It's really me," I say.

"Was that you speaking to me on the comm a few nights ago?"

"Yes."

"Why didn't you tell me then?" he asks.

"People were listening. And they're watching right now. I'll explain everything later. But I just—I had to let you know."

"Audie, this is . . . it's—"

"I know," I tell him. "Believe me. I've been living like this for days."

"But how did it happen? What did you—"

"Come *on*, then!" Sarah calls out to us. "Where's your sense of urgency?"

"Please," I whisper to Daniel. "Just wait. We'll talk about everything as soon as we're alone. But for now you have to pretend nothing's wrong. Can you do that?"

"No," he says, "I can't."

"Try," I say. "And *smile*. I'm your good friend Halli, and you're happy to see me—right?"

"Where do you think she is?" he asks. "And where is the rest of—" He gestures at Halli's body. "—you?"

I slap him on the arm and say loudly enough for everyone to hear, "It's good to see you, too, Daniel. Now let's go do what your sister wants."

"Finally!" Sarah says. "Someone is speaking sense."

As we turn around and head back to the group, Daniel lays his hand lightly against my back. It's just a gesture, something small, but I see Jake notice it. And then he looks at me.

I step away from Daniel.

This is going to be just as hard as I thought.

34

It's a small gathering, just the five of us and two of Sarah's friends, and at least there's enough conversation going on that no one expects Daniel to say much, which is good, since he's barely said five words. He reminds me of me, that morning on the plane last week when my brain was so busy processing everything, I couldn't come up with even the smallest of small talk. Daniel and I need to go somewhere alone—soon. That's all there is to it.

We're at a kind of café, someplace cozy and out of the way, so even though people are looking at me, there aren't too many of them. I've boosted my caffeine with three more cups of this dark, rich coffee, so maybe that's enough to get me through the night.

Because I have the feeling it's going to be a long time

before I get some sleep. Daniel and I have a lot of figuring out to do.

Jake has made sure to sit close to me—not so close that people would think we're an item, but close enough that he's reminding *me* of that—and I can see Daniel sees that, too.

I'll tell him it's all part of the act—me being Halli. Although I'm not sure he'll believe it any more than I do.

"Where did you go to school?" Sarah is asking Bryan. "Somewhere in the States?"

"No, I've been apprenticed since I was young," Bryan answers. "Cameras, holofilming, sound production, locations—my dad's done it for years, so he got me in."

And that's the first time I've thought of it: I've been so absorbed by my own situation, I never really paid much attention to what was going on with Jake and his siblings.

"Did you go to school?" I ask Jake quietly.

He pops another handful of ginger-crusted peanuts into his mouth. "No, your father took me on when I was fifteen."

"So, what did you do before then?" I ask.

"I helped with the stables, mostly," he says. "Some work in the house—whatever needed doing. I'd take over Lyman's duties whenever he needed to leave."

I can't picture Jake as the doorman. I wonder if he had to wear the black jacket and white gloves.

"So Celeste doesn't go to school, either?" I ask.

Jake is looking at me funny now. Like I should know better than to ask these questions.

"I mean, no," I say, "obviously not. She's working." I cough and take a sip of coffee.

I catch Daniel's eye. He's sitting across the table, which is inconvenient, since usually whenever I got into situations like this he'd sit beside me and bump my leg with his or squeeze my hand—something to let me know I'm doing something wrong that's going to get me exposed.

But I'm curious now, and so I'm going to keep going. Carefully.

"When did Alexa start working for my mother?"

"Same time," Jake says. "Fifteen."

"What will Celeste do?" I ask. "When she's fifteen?"

"She wants to graduate from house maid to assistant cook." Jake laughs. "If you can believe it, she'd rather work for my mother than Alexa."

"Oh. Right," I say. "Sure."

There's something that still doesn't make sense: if Jake has only been apprenticed to Halli's father for the past two years, how did he learn so much chemistry? Because it was clear in our meeting with Mr. Chilton that Jake knows as much about it as I do—maybe more.

"So how did you learn chemistry?" I ask him. "Just from my father?"

"No, from the histories," Jake says.

And now Bryan, who I thought was too preoccupied listening to Sarah, turns to us and chimes in.

"Which ones?" he asks Jake. "Two or seven?"

"Two," Jake answers. "I always liked theirs best."

"Too technical," Bryan says. "Seven's better—more stories."

I steal a glance at Daniel. He's too far away to explain this all to me.

"What about fourteen?" Sarah asks. "Surely the finest history organization of all time, and before you answer it's my duty to tell you that Daniel's and my parents work there, so your correct answer must be unequivocal admiration."

"History 14 is the best," Bryan says, "by far."

Sarah extends her hand. "You may now claim me in marriage. My parents will not object."

Bryan kisses the top of her hand and he . . . is . . . gone. If that isn't the expression of a guy who's totally smitten—

Sarah sighs. "I envy you two," she says to Jake and Bryan. "I've *begged* my parents to apprentice me instead of always sending me back to that medieval school, but since I have no discernable talent at anything useful, it's been difficult for me to tell them precisely what it is I want to *do*."

"Theater!" one of her friends, the girl with short blonde hair says.

"Yes, well, one can only play Marie Curie discovering radium so many times, can't one?" Sarah answers. "What I'm really hoping is that Halli Markham will allow me to apprentice myself to her, so she can teach me to be an explorer."

"Oh . . . uh . . . seriously?" I ask.

"That depends," Sarah says, "on whether you take the request seriously." She smiles. "If not, then of course I'm joking."

But I see it on her face: that hopeful look.

"Um, let me think about it, okay?" I have no idea what else to say. Would Halli ever take on an apprentice? And what, exactly, would that mean?

"What about you, Dan?" Jake asks, addressing him directly for the first time all evening. "School or profession?"

"School," Daniel says. "For now. "I haven't been fortunate to find an apprenticeship in my field."

"Which is?" Jake asks, pleasantly enough. Although I can hear a particular tone underneath it.

"Neurobotany," Sarah answers for her brother. "Loads more difficult than any one of us at this table will ever understand, so I suggest we move on to the discussion of food. You don't mind, do you, Daniel?"

"Not at all," he says, tilting his head in a kind of formal nod toward Jake. Like he's acknowledging some unspoken challenge between the two of them.

"Good," Sarah says, "because tea and scones were a fine start, but I need something more substantial, and clearly Bryan does, too, since he's already eaten everyone else's share."

For a moment Bryan looks embarrassed.

"I like a man with a hardy appetite," Sarah says. "It means he'll hold his tongue someday when I get old and fat, since he'll be even older and fatter. How old are you?"

"Twenty-two," Bryan answers.

"Yes, then, see?" Sarah says. "Five years advance start. Eat however much you like. You know what your future holds."

Bryan turns to Daniel. "Is your sister like this with everyone?"

"She's usually very shy," Daniel answers. "Can barely speak. We've had to hire tutors to force her to recite the alphabet."

I'm relieved to hear him be sarcastic. That's the Daniel I know. Maybe he's over the shock.

"We go to an all-girls school," Sarah's brunette friend tells Bryan. "Don't worry—she hardly meets anyone."

"And this one's obviously taken by Halli Markham," Sarah says, pointing to Jake. "So that leaves you and me, Bryan . . ."

She says a few more witty things, and Bryan says a few back, but I'm stuck in this vortex right here, feeling Daniel's eyes boring into me, feeling Jake tense at my side, and noticing that even though Bryan didn't miss a beat and kept on talking, his expression changed ever so slightly in that moment as he took note of a potentially juicy piece of gossip.

I love Sarah, but sometimes . . .

"Oh, if only your cousin could be here!" she says to me. "Think of how much more fun we'd have! Daniel, don't you miss Audie?"

"Terribly," he says, looking straight into my eyes.

35

"Miss Markham," the doorman says with a slight bow.

"Hi, Bates."

"You're not really going to go with them, are you?" Jake asks as we head for the elevator.

"I have to," I say. "Sarah's family is expecting me." Which isn't quite true, since I'm not even sure her parents know she invited me to stay. But it's exactly the kind of excuse I need so I can grab some time alone with Daniel and start sorting this whole thing out.

This whole physics thing, I mean. I'm not sure at all what to do about the personal.

Bryan is still in the car. I could tell when we got out that he wasn't quite ready to let Sarah out of his sight for the night. I've seen her charm a guy before—this schoolmate of Daniel's who came along with them to the Alps—but that was nothing compared to this all-out flirtation with Bryan. Or maybe Bryan is just better at the game than Martin was, and Sarah is enjoying herself that much more. I'm sure I'll get the story once we've moved onto the slumber party stage of the night.

But first I have this stage to get through. The part where I keep Jake over there and me over here, and not fall back into our habit lately of making out whenever no one else is around.

The latest demonstration of that was when we were in Mr. Chilton's office this afternoon, going over some of the holographic diagrams I asked him to show me. Bryan was still banned from the room since we were talking about corporate secrets, and at one point Mr. Chilton had to leave for a few minutes to answer a call.

Jake held his finger to his lips, maybe because he knew the walls were bugged, just like the bedrooms on the island, then he pulled me to him and starting kissing me as quietly as a person can kiss while also making the other person dizzy and halfway out of her mind. And then we heard Mr. Chilton at the door, and quickly pulled apart and went back to discussing chemistry.

And the thing is, by then I already knew I'd probably see Daniel tonight, and I was already thinking how that would feel to be around him again, and I knew I'd probably feel guilty with Jake there, so I decided to try to keep away from Jake for the next couple of days, or however long I'll be with Daniel. And so it was perfect when Sarah invited me to stay at their house, because I thought that way I'd never have to be alone with Jake for the rest of the trip.

Not counting on those stolen moments while a Chief Operating Officer leaves the room.

Or this moment, returning to the flat so I can pack.

"So," Jake says, "who is he?"

He's just opened the door and let us both into the flower room, and the scent is as overpowering as ever. I won't miss sleeping here tonight.

"Who—Daniel?" I say in my most innocent-sounding voice.

I head into the bedroom to repack Halli's duffel. Red hops up on the bed and nestles into the pile of pillows. Jake follows us in.

"You know who he is," I say. "He's Sarah's brother. Isn't she great? Did you see how Bryan was looking at her all ni—"

"No," Jake clarifies, "who is he to *you?*"

I'm prepared for the question. I've been thinking about it the whole ride back from the café. Because I knew Jake was probably going to ask me something like this, and I also suspect he's going to ask me about someone else at some point, and so I might as well handle both questions right now with the same lie.

"He's just a friend," I say. "He likes this girl Audie we all met in the Alps."

"Your cousin," Jake says.

I force a laugh. "Yeah, right. Sarah kept calling her that because she thought we were so much alike. She was a nice girl—Audie, I mean. Daniel really liked her."

Have I covered everything? I think so.

But apparently Jake doesn't think so. "It looked like you two were pretty friendly when you first saw each other this afternoon."

"Well, Daniel's a friendly guy. And I had a message for him from Audie—that's what I whispered in his ear."

Now have I covered everything?

"So you're staying in his house," Jake says, "but there's nothing going on."

"I'm staying in his *parents'* house, in his sister's room, and no, there's nothing going on."

"Good." Jake draws me away from my packing, and turns me around to face him. He tucks my hair behind one ear and looks into my eyes. Then he slips his hand behind my neck and brushes his lips against my cheek. "Because you know that would break my heart," he whispers, kissing my cheek, my jaw, my lips.

And by the time he gets there, forget it. All my high-minded plans go out the window. And now my arms are around him, my fingers twisted in his hair, my mouth bruising against his, and as far as I'm concerned, we can go on like this for the next five hours and I'll be in no hurry to stop.

But then we hear a *POP!* and immediately pull apart.

Bryan is sitting in the outer room, sprawled across one of the flowery chairs. When we come back out there he lifts his glass to both of us.

"Champagne?" he asks. "I know you don't drink, Miss Markham, but you might want some for this."

"For what?" I ask, looking at Jake. It's clear we've both been kissing. We both look disheveled.

"We're going to have a discussion, the three of us," Bryan says. "Off the record, to begin with."

"About what?" Jake asks.

"About the story I'm going to tell," Bryan answers. "About the two of you. Because it's going to get out, and it's my exclusive—that's the deal.

"So have a seat," he tells us. "Start talking."

36

"Oh, and don't worry about Daniel and Sarah," Bryan tells me. "The driver is taking them home. He'll come back for you in an hour. We have plenty of time."

Then he looks at Jake and me with the pleasantest of smiles, like we're all just having a chat and isn't this lovely.

And I don't really see what else to do. So I take the sofa, and Jake takes a chair.

"Do your parents know?" Bryan asks me.

"No," I say. "Absolutely not. They'd fire Jake if they knew."

If I have to lie my way through this, I'm going to *lie*.

"When did it start?" Bryan asks.

"A few days ago," I say.

"Nine years," Jake answers. "I've loved her since I was eight."

Oh, so we're telling *that* kind of a story.

"Miss Markham—may I call you Halli?"

"You might as well," I say. It seems like we're past any formality now.

"Halli, how long have you loved Jake?"

"Uh..."

"Do you love him?" Bryan presses.

I stand back up. "Look, this is really personal. I'm not very comfortable with it. There are some things that are just private."

I look to Jake for support. But he's not saying a word.

"I told you you could film me," I go on, "but I never said anything about answering a bunch of personal questions."

"Someone is going to ask them," Bryan answers. "Wouldn't you rather it was me?"

"Why is 'someone' going to ask them?" I say. "What makes you think anyone will know? We can be more careful—can't we, Jake?"

Bryan turns to him. "Sarah noticed. Other people will, too. It's my fault I'm so dense, or I would have picked up on it sooner. Do you want someone like History 1 breaking it? It'll be far worse."

Jake groans. "He's right," he tells me.

"But I don't *want* this," I say, and I know I sound like

I'm whining, but I really don't see why I have to do what these guys say. Halli is entitled to her own life. Why does she have to bow to pressure to let anyone film her at all?

So that's what I decide to do: just pull the plug.

"This interview is over," I say. "I'm sorry, Bryan, but you'll have to leave. I'm sure Hal—" I almost say "Halli's" again. "—my parents will fly you back home, and they'll pay you for your time."

Bryan doesn't budge. He just looks at me calmly. "It doesn't work that way, Halli. This is history. History is a fact. So either decide how you want the facts to come out, or someone else is going to decide for you. Me, or someone else."

I look to Jake for help.

"History 1 would be worse," he says. "A lot worse. I think we need to go with Bryan."

"There are no facts to tell," I say, going to the bedroom to retrieve Halli's duffel and her dog. We both come back and head for the door. "Nothing's going on and nothing will. Jake, thank you for helping me these past few days. It was nice meeting you."

Then I open the door and flee into the hall, skipping the elevator to run down the stairs. Halli's lungs and legs handle it well, and I'm barely out of breath by the time I reach the bottom.

"Can you call my driver back?" I ask Bates. "Is there any way to reach him?"

"Certainly, Miss. Where shall I—"

"I'll be waiting outside," I say, as I watch the elevator coming down. "And do me a favor—try to keep Jake here as long as you can. That's an order—if you don't mind."

Then Red and I take off through the doors and head out into the dark and hope no one will follow.

37

I'm not even sure what my problem is. What's the big deal? So what if some reporter does a piece on Halli being in love with some guy who works for her parents? What difference does it make to me? It's not my life. And would the real Halli even care? Or would she just laugh about it?

I'm crouched down, hiding in this little alcove with Red, a few buildings away from where the flat is. People are passing by, going home or on their way out, and I watch between their weaving legs, switching off between looking at the door to the apartment building to see if anyone comes out, and watching the street to see if the car has arrived yet so Red and I can just leap in and make a fast getaway.

I really expected to see Jake or even Bryan come out

after me, but maybe Bates is doing what I asked and holding them in there. Good. Thank you. Perfect.

"Halli?"

I let out a little yelp.

The whole time I was watching the doors, Jake must have gone out a different way and looped around the block. He's come at me from a totally different direction.

"Where's . . . Bryan?"

"He's back in the flat," Jake says. "Don't worry."

I'm still crouched down, in traditional hiding mode. Jake sits on the sidewalk in front of me. He reaches over and pets Red. The dog's tail thumps.

"I'm sorry about that," he says. "All of it. It's my fault —I should have been more careful."

"What do you want to do?" I ask.

"Nothing. Let him say what he wants to say."

"Seriously? But what if it's bad?"

Jake shrugs.

"Would my parents fire you?" I ask. "I was just making that up, but—is it true?"

"I don't know," he says. "I don't really care."

"How can you not care?"

There's light coming from the lobby of the building next door, and it's enough to let me see Jake's face. And enough for him to see mine. He looks me in the eyes.

"Why do you think I've been working for your father all this time?" he asks. "I could have gone somewhere else. I could have left that place a long time ago."

I can feel the saliva in my mouth drying up. Because I think I know where this is going. And I think it might just scare me.

"I've been waiting for you," Jake tells me. "I didn't know how else to do it. So I've just been biding my time there, hoping some day you'd finally show up."

"Oh, Jake—"

He stops petting Red and reaches for my hand.

"I understand you not wanting to say it in front of some reporter, but . . ."

I close my eyes. This can not be happening. Some guy I'm way too attracted to for my own good is asking me whether I love him. And he's not asking me, he's asking Halli.

"Miss Markham?"

And now the driver is here. Of course. And Sarah and Daniel are in the back. They must not have made it all the way home before Bates was able to reach them.

"Just tell me," Jake whispers. "I need to know."

I cover my face with my hand. He gently pries it away.

And with nowhere else to hide, I have to tell him the truth:

"Yes, I think I do."

38

"Well, he's certainly dreamy, isn't he?" Sarah asks as soon as I get in the car. Red hops onto the seat next to her and rests his head on her lap. She seems to have that effect on all males.

"Now," Sarah says, "tell us absolutely everything about you and this Jake person, and don't leave out any of the good parts. Unless they'd embarrass Daniel, in which case, Daniel, I'll have to ask you to leap out of the vehicle. Driver, go slowly."

The car interior is too dark for me to see either of them clearly, but I can feel Daniel's eyes on me.

"There's nothing to tell," I say. "He works for my parents. They sent him as an escort."

"Why can't our parents ever send me with an escort

who looks like that?" Sarah asks. "It's always either Daniel or our Aunt Miriam."

"So what about you and Bryan?" I say, ready to change the subject. "You two looked pretty happy together."

"Nice bloke, good hair—we shall see," she says.

"How long have you known him?" Daniel asks me.

"Just a couple of days," I say. "He was the reporter at a board—"

"No," Daniel says, "Jake." His voice isn't his regular voice. There's a flat sort of deadness to it.

"Oh. Since last week," I say. "He showed up at . . . my house," I almost said Halli's, "to pick me up and take me to my parents."

"So you've finally met the delinquent parents!" Sarah says. "Oh, that must have been rich. I wish I could have seen it. Did our Bryan film it?"

I'm not surprised she'd ask. Sarah's grown up watching film clips of Halli. It probably seems natural to her that every aspect of Halli's life will eventually be on view.

"Not the initial meeting," I say. "But he was at a board meeting later."

"Bored, indeed," Sarah complains. "Who cares about that? We want to have seen the look on your parents' faces when confronted with the child they abandoned and neglected. And the look on your face—were you very stern with them, then? Oh, I wish I could have seen it!"

"Sarah—" Daniel warns.

"What? Can't we speak freely? We're all friends here, aren't we, Halli?"

"We are, and it's fine," I tell them. "I don't mind."

But it's nice of Daniel to try to rein his sister in, just in case it might hurt Halli's feelings.

But he knows I'm not Halli, so that can't be the reason.

"I hope we didn't interrupt anything important just now," Daniel says. "Between you and Jake."

"No, nothing important," I say. Daniel wasn't trying to spare my feelings, he just wanted to return to a topic he's more interested in.

"You seemed to be very involved when we drove up," he says. "Perhaps you wish we'd driven on and left you two alone."

"Daniel, you sound as though you're jealous!" Sarah says. "This is Halli Markham, remember? Not the other cousin. How is Audie?" she asks me. "Why isn't she here? She's coming for our father's party, isn't she?"

"I don't think she can make it, Sarah. I'm sorry."

"No! Unacceptable!" she says. "Not when my brother's been pining for her night and day since he saw her last!"

"Sarah—" he says.

"No, Daniel, I'm quite serious. You've been wretched to live with. Dear Halli, can't you please help my poor, love-starved brother? He simply *has* to see her again. Can't you assemble a brigade of some sort to kidnap her wherever she is and bring her here?"

My eyes have adjusted to the dark by now, and Daniel and I can both see each other clearly. He gives me a sad sort of chuckle and looks away. Not like he's angry, but more like he's embarrassed.

"I'll try," I say. "I agree. She should be here. We should all be here."

"Quite correct," Sarah says. "Oh, look—we're almost there. Now, hide here for a moment while Daniel and I go in first. We haven't told our parents you're staying yet—you're meant to be a surprise. They think they're not meeting you until the party. They're simply going to die of admiration when they see you walk through our door! Ready, Dan?"

Sarah exits first, and I catch Daniel's arm.

"I'm sorry," I tell him. "Really sorry. Everything is so messed up right now."

"I'm certain that's true," he says.

"Where can we talk? When? I have so much I have to tell you."

Sarah has come running back. "Daniel! Come *on*! Halli, wait two minutes—"

"I look forward to it," Daniel tells me in a very

formal kind of way, then he exits the car. He follows Sarah up the walkway into a narrow, two-story house.

I watch the two of them go in. The place looks cozy, well-lit, warm. I'm sure the people inside—most of them, at least—will happily welcome me.

I lean forward and cradle my head in my hands. What am I doing here? Everything has gotten so out of hand. The whole point of coming to London was to see Daniel—to talk to him. To find out everything he knows and have him help me get Halli back. Everything else—visiting Halli's parents' facility, having Jake and some reporter tag along—those were supposed to be just an excuse, a way to make it happen.

But it's all turned around. A few days ago, I thought the hard part would be getting here in the first place. Now I know the hard part starts right now, through those doors, with Daniel.

And it's nobody's fault but mine. I've lost my focus. I've gotten so caught up with Jake, I've completely lost my mind and forgotten what I'm supposed to do.

"Will you be staying, Miss Markham?" the driver asks me. I never caught his name.

"Yes," I answer. "At least for tonight."

"Very good, Miss." He leaves the car door he's been holding open, and goes to the back to retrieve my duffel. Then he takes up his station again and waits for me to come out.

Two minutes surely must have passed. I wouldn't

mind making it ten minutes more. I have no strategy. I didn't think I'd need one. It's Daniel. He and I should be able to talk easily, effortlessly.

I see the front door open. Sarah is wildly gesturing for me.

"Come on, Red," I say. "Show time."

39

I am sitting at a table in a cramped little kitchen—
even smaller than the one my mom and I share at
home—and I'm surrounded by people all talking at
once, laughing, debating in a good-natured way, obviously enjoying each other's company, and we're eating
leftovers and drinking tea and having a grand old time
except for one thing: Daniel politely excused himself a
little while ago and hasn't come back.

He's not the kind of guy to do it for effect—he's not
pouting, hoping to make some statement—I think he's
just being honest with himself right now about the fact
that he doesn't want to be around me.

Which is a horrible, horrible fact, and not one I
want to let go on for one more second. This is ridiculous. I have to fix it.

"Do you guys mind?" I ask. "I just remembered I need to ask Daniel something. Is it okay if I go find him?"

"Upstairs," his mother, Francie, tells me. Both Daniel's parents told me to call them by their first names. "Third door on the right," she says. Then she and Sarah and the dad, Sam, go back to arguing whether some food I've never heard of tastes better mashed or chopped, and which ancient civilization first discovered it. Sarah says chopped and Persian, her parents think mashed and Incan. That's how the whole conversation has been tonight—a mixture of the modern and the historical. It's pretty funny to listen to. Even when I was one of their topics.

"No, that was the year she and her grandmother first trekked to the Arctic—remember?" Sarah asked.

"Are you sure?" Sam said. "I thought that was when they were in India—wasn't that the year with the tiger?"

Sarah looked exasperated. "I wrote a report about it for school. Of course I remember."

And since I didn't know the answers to any of their trivia questions about Halli, I just let them all hash it out, and sat here with a mysterious smile on my face.

But now it's time for facing Daniel, which might even be harder than facing a tiger. I excuse myself from the table and head upstairs with Red.

The carpeting on the floors looks worn, but the

place is clean. Cluttered, but clean. A lot like my house, with too much stuff stuffed into every room.

Daniel's door is closed. I knock.

"Yes?"

I open the door. He's sitting on his bed, reading a book. It's been a while since I've seen one of those—everything here seems to run on tablets.

"Can I come in?"

"Of course."

There's no place to sit, really, except on the bed or on the floor, and even though Daniel would probably be more comfortable with me standing, it's time to break the ice. I sit down on the edge of his bed, a decent distance away from him, and pat the space between us for Red to jump up and fill.

There's no point in pretending. In pretending about anything.

"Do you hate me?" I ask.

"No. Of course not." Daniel closes his book and sets it aside. "Of course I don't hate you."

"You saw."

"Yes," he says, "I saw."

"He thinks I'm Halli," I say, as if that answers every-thing. But since we're not pretending, I know it doesn't.

"What are your feelings for him?" Daniel asks.

"Confused."

He nods. And takes that in.

"He's in love with Halli," I say. "He's constantly trying to win her over."

"Which it seems he has," Daniel says.

"But I'm not Halli," I say. "I don't want to be Halli. I don't know if she's alive or whether I can still save her, but I have to do everything I can. And I'm hoping you'll help me. It's why I'm here. I came all the way to England just to talk to you. Everything else . . . doesn't really matter. You have to believe me about that."

And I have to believe it myself. Because otherwise everything I'm doing is a waste, and whether or not Halli survives becomes unimportant compared to my love life.

And that's not how I want it to be. I know if she were in my place, she'd be working night and day to find me, to bring me back. She wouldn't be hanging out in cafés and hotel rooms just letting the hours and days tick by. I've already let too much time slip away. It's all starting to hit me right now, and I'm getting a little panicked.

Besides, it's not just Halli—I want myself back, too. No matter how much I might enjoy a few moments here and there inside this body, particularly when Jake is around. It's time for me to go back to my own life. I want that. I think I forgot that.

And part of my old life is in front of me.

"I'm sorry about everything," I tell Daniel. "This isn't how I wanted it. The last time I saw you, I couldn't wait to see you again. And this afternoon, when you first showed up, the way I felt . . . that's how I want it. I'm sorry, Daniel. I'm sorry for all of it."

And that, I know, is the truth. It's like I've just woken up from a trance.

Daniel studies my face. Then he takes a deep breath. He props himself up against the wall behind him and makes more room for me and the dog.

"All right," he says, "let's hear it. All of it. Start from the beginning."

And even though Sarah barges in several times over the next few hours—"Come downstairs! What are you two about?" "It's my turn now, Dan. She was meant to be in my room." "Invite your own friends! Halli Markham is mine"—Daniel and I don't budge. We'll sit here all night if we have to, even if it means I never get to sleep again.

Because this is science now, and we're not leaving until we figure it out.

40

"Audie." Daniel is gently shaking me awake.

I'm bent over, half of me still in a sitting position on his bed, half of me slumped to the side. I think Daniel must have fallen asleep, too, because I don't remember hearing his voice for however long I've been passed out. It might have been fifteen minutes, it might have been an hour.

Sunlight is streaming through the curtains. It's not exactly like waking up in a simulated meadow, with a deer grazing nearby, or in a room overpoweringly scented with roses, but I think this kind of room suits me better. Reminds me of home. Reminds who I really am underneath all this.

"I think Red needs to go out," I say. He's standing by the door, wagging his tail.

Daniel stands up and stretches. "I'll go with you."

My teeth feel like they're coated in wax. My tongue, too. I could use a good tooth brushing and a long, hot shower. But my duffel is in Sarah's room, and I don't want to wake her up to get my toothbrush, so for now I'll have to make do with the cup of tea Francie hands me when we come downstairs to the kitchen.

Daniel's father is sitting there, too. Only Sarah is missing.

"She had to leave already," Francie tells me. "Her school has an early start."

"Not yours?" I ask Daniel.

"Not today," he says.

The air is frosty outside—much cooler than it's been —and as usual I don't have the proper clothes. But Daniel lends me a thick coat of his and finds some gloves that belong to Sarah, and the two of us set off with Red to stretch all of our legs.

"Any new thoughts?" I ask Daniel. "I thought maybe with a little sleep . . ."

"A few," he says. "But it's too early yet. Let me wake up."

A wet fog covers the ground, misting around our shins. Red lopes along, running ahead, coming back, staying near us but still enjoying his freedom. It's not like walking on the beach with someone who will throw him a stick, but it's still fresh air, and it's morning, and both of those make him frisky.

We walk for a long time. Up small streets, across a busy one where Daniel has to save me from being hit by a car because I forgot to look the wrong way again, then finally to a grassy park where Red is happy to chase the British version of squirrels. There's even a pond with a few cold-tolerant ducks in it, and Red, who seems oblivious to freezing water, jumps in to investigate. Then when he notices Daniel and I have walked on, he splashes out to find us and ends up shaking himself dry in just the right spot to soak both of our legs through our clothes. You can take a dog across the ocean, but he still doesn't know how to behave.

"Shouldn't you be going to school?" I ask Daniel, realizing how late it must be.

"I won't be going today. Today I think we need to visit my parents' studio."

I already confessed to Daniel last night how awful I feel for wasting so much time—time I should have spent thinking my hardest about how to solve the physics of my problem—and now visiting his parents seems like more of the same.

I tell him so.

"No, I think it will help," he says. "I have an idea. It might be totally wrong, but it's all I can think of right now. But you're going to have to trust me."

"I do trust you," I say.

"Right, then," he answers. "We should go back home

now. You're going to have to start by telling my parents."

"Telling them what?" I ask, more than a little alarmed.

"Everything," Daniel says. "Everything from before—from when we first met—and everything now."

"But . . . why?" It seems crazy. Bringing someone else in at this point—trying to convince Daniel's parents that what's been happening in my life the past month or so isn't a dream, isn't a fantasy, but involves highly complex and sometimes impossible to understand physics, seems like another huge waste of time.

And it might create more problems than it can ever solve, if, for example, Daniel's parents come to the same kind of conclusion Jake has—that what I really have is a head injury or a mental problem, and I belong in a hospital, not in a parallel universe.

"I can't do it," I tell Daniel. "I think that's a big mistake."

"Do you trust me?" he asks again.

I groan.

"Do you?"

"Yes, Daniel. Of course I trust you."

"Then come on," he says. "I have a plan. Let's test whether it has any hope of working."

41

There's a car sitting in front of Daniel's house. A car I recognize.

The windows are shaded dark, so I can't see in from outside, but I know who'll be sitting in the back seat.

"I'll . . . meet you in there," I tell Daniel.

He looks at me, and I can imagine what he's thinking. But he just responds with a nod and turns up the walk to his house.

I stand outside the car. The window closest to me rolls down.

"Get in," Jake says. "You must be freezing."

"I have to go back inside," I tell him. "I can't stay out here long."

"Halli," he says, giving me that familiar, nearly-irresistible smile, "get in."

I glance back toward the house, but Daniel has already gone inside.

"Just for a moment," I say, opening the door.

Red is happy to jump in and reunite with his stick-throwing buddy.

There's a barrier up between the back seat and the front, so the driver can't see us. It wasn't there last night when I rode in this car. Jake obviously knows where the controls are.

I sit at a respectable distance, but that doesn't last long. Jake has me halfway onto his side of the seat in no time.

"I haven't brushed my—"

But obviously he doesn't care. And a few moments later, I don't, either.

"I missed you," Jake says when we finally need to breathe. "Come back with me. We can go explore London today. I know a place you'll—"

"I can't. I have things to do here."

"What things?" he wants to know. "You were here all night."

"I just need a few days," I say. "I'm here for a visit. I can't leave yet—Sarah will be disappointed."

He strokes his finger down my cheek. "What about me? I'll be disappointed."

I can't believe I'm so weak. This isn't how I wanted things to go. It was easier to think about all of this clearly when I wasn't within inches from Jake. It's like

I've passed over the event horizon of a black hole, and the force of him is pulling me in, too powerful to fight.

"Halli . . ." he whispers, about to kiss me again.

Halli. Exactly. Halli. I'm here for her, not me.

"I have to go." I hit the handle and fling open the car door and get out before I can think again. Or before I can stop thinking again.

"Come on, Red." The dog doesn't want to budge. He's stuck in Jake's gravitational pull, too.

I finally coax the dog out. "Just give me a few days," I tell Jake. "I'll . . . call you somehow. I'll come find you. But please, I need these few days alone."

He looks confused, and I don't blame him. Didn't I just tell him that I loved him last night?

"Please, Jake. I'm sorry. I—I have to go."

Then I slam the door shut and run up the walk before I can change my mind.

Please let me find Halli again. And let her come back and sort out this life.

42

I'm sitting at the kitchen table in the Everett-Wheeler home, trying my best to describe as simply as I can everything that's happened since I first had that breakthrough meditation on a Saturday morning and ended up over here in this universe, up on a mountain ridge, staring at the parallel version of me.

And then I give them Part 2, the whole description I gave Daniel last night about everything that's happened since last Thursday.

Daniel's parents are mostly quiet through the whole thing, not asking a lot of questions, and in a way it reminds me of when I first told Daniel everything about how I managed to bridge the gap between our two universes and why it was I kept disappearing at such inconvenient times. He didn't freak out on me. He just sat there with his head in his hands part of the time, listening hard, really trying to comprehend.

His parents take it even better than he did, just sipping lots of tea, nodding a lot, making me pause for a few minutes while Francie makes more toast because she says she's suddenly ravenously hungry and can't possibly listen anymore until she has some bread and jam in her, then once that's done I get to continue on.

It probably only takes about an hour, all told, and then the four of us sit back in our chairs and take a breather and just look at each other.

And after a few silent minutes like that, Francie finally says, "Yes. Well." And then a little more time goes by before she says, "It's possible Sam and I can help you."

"Help me?" I say. "How?"

"Has Daniel told you what we do?" his mother asks.

"Um, not exactly. I mean, I know you're an archaeologist, and Sam is a history producer, but that's about it."

Daniel's parents exchange a look. Then his mother smiles. "Shall I tell you the story of our first meeting?"

"Coffee this time, Audie?" Daniel asks me, getting up to make it. Every time he calls me Audie is just feels SO good. Like someone has finally scratched this itch in the middle of my back that I haven't been able to reach.

But it's strange that they're all so casual right now. I mean, I just shared with them a shocking story of physics gone wrong, and instead of asking me a bunch of questions about that, his parents want to tell me the story of their romance?

But they've just indulged me for the last hour, so the least I can do is listen to them, even though the truth is I'm much more interested in Francie's statement that she and her husband might be able to help me.

"I was nineteen," Francie says. "Sam was twenty-two. I'd graduated the year before from the same girls' school Sarah attends now, and instead of attending university, I had the good fortune of being apprenticed to one of my former instructors. Her name was Carolyn Brown, and she'd recently left teaching to return to the field.

"She was a famous archaeologist—perhaps you've heard of her?"

Francie laughs at herself. "No, sorry, I forgot—you're not from here. Dr. Brown was a wonderful woman—still is—I don't mean to imply she's passed on or anything, she's simply retired. She still comes for holidays, doesn't she, Daniel?"

"I have the souvenir socks to prove it," he says.

"She brings you socks?" I ask.

"From all over the world. Began when I was just a little boy. Can't seem to stop her now."

"You love those!" his mother says.

"Yes, I'm wearing a pair right now," Daniel says, meanwhile shaking his head "no" at me.

"In any case," Francie continues, "Dr. Brown was my

mentor. She taught me everything I know about everything having to do with artifacts, burial sites, preserving ancient remains—all of it."

"Get on with the love story," Sam tells her. "How we saw each other across a crowded dig site, you fancied me immediately..."

"Yes, yes," his wife says. "All true." Then she mimics the same thing Daniel just did, shaking her head at me "no."

Daniel gets up to pour me a mug of coffee. Then he sits back down beside me, slightly closer than before. The chill I felt from him when I first came back in, after sitting in the car with Jake, seems gone now. I think we're back to being friends.

It helped that he had such a big part to play in the story I told his parents about everything that's gone on. There's no denying Daniel has been a significant part of my life over here.

"And why were you there, darling?" Francie asks her husband. "What was so newsworthy about a group of dusty archaeologists roaming some remote, featureless desert?"

Sam leans across the table and looks me intently in the eyes. "Because it was the first time anyone had openly brought a clairvoyant along on a dig."

"A . . . clairvoyant?" I ask. "As in . . ."

"Able to see what we cannot see," Sam says. "See beyond what's apparent to our five senses."

"Like a psychic," I say.

"Yes," Sam says. "Just so. We don't use that term so much, but you and I are speaking of the same thing."

"Why did you bring a clairvoyant?" I ask.

"Because Dr. Brown had tired of the game," Francie says. "Of pretending that other tools didn't exist. She wanted to be the first archaeologist to acknowledge the contributions that can be made by people with extraordinary abilities."

"So . . . what did this person do?" I ask.

"This person was a farmer named John Thornton," Francie tells me. "A wonderful, quiet man, very little education, large, generous heart. He had lived with his ability all his life, and had hidden it away from everyone, including his wife.

"But then one day, when the two of them were visiting a farm they were considering purchasing, Mr. Thornton stopped in the middle of the field, pointed at the ground, and said, 'There's a wall here. Straight down.' He began walking very quickly, pacing out the dimensions of something he could see so clearly in his mind, even though his wife and the other farmer could see nothing but dirt clods and grass.

"Mr. Thornton was so excited," Francie goes on, "he forgot to hide his knowledge. He spoke freely for the first time of what he saw: a wall, a deep pit, an ancient cremation site and burial ground."

"Did they believe him?" I ask.

"Eventually," she says. "He was so adamant that the land contained this ancient site, he made a wager with the other farmer: if a crew of men with shovels dug downward in one specific spot, exactly as far as Mr. Thornton instructed, and thereby discovered this wall that he could see so clearly in his mind, then the other farmer would sell the land to Mr. Thornton and his wife at a reduced price. If the dig yielded nothing, Mr. Thornton would pay double."

"But he got his discount," I say.

"He did indeed," Francie says. "And word began to spread. Until finally it reached the ears of my mentor, who persuaded Mr. Thornton to join us in our work."

"But you didn't inform any of the history organizations right away," Sam says.

"No," Francie agrees. "We wanted to be certain—Dr. Brown wanted that. She didn't want us all to be made fools. So we asked Mr. Thornton to accompany us on several digs we'd arranged over a period of months. And he was right every time."

"Right, how?" I ask.

"He always knew what lay beneath the ground," Francie says. "Exactly what it was, and where it was. Buildings, pottery, bones—can you imagine, Audie, how much time and effort he saved us, simply by walking a stretch of ground and directing us exactly where to dig?"

"I can see that," I say. "What a great idea."

"Then once we were certain," Francie says, "we called in the histories."

"Called all of them," Sam says. "But no one was interested."

"Not no one," Francie says. "There was this one young gentleman. Very eager, I recall. Willing to listen to a young woman with a strange tale."

Sam shrugs. "It was a slow week."

Francie smiles. "It was destiny. Sam flew out with us to a site in Egypt. He was there when Mr. Thornton walked the desert floor, describing everything beneath it. And Sam stayed on while we began excavation and discovered the first of many of the structures and artifacts that Mr. Thornton had described."

"And by then," Sam says, "everyone with eyes could see how much Francie had taken a fancy to me, so I had to propose to her to spare her reputation."

"He proposed ten days in," Francie says. "I said no. He proposed two more times over the course of the trip before I took pity on the man."

"They married within two months of meeting each other," Daniel tells me. "They're both clearly irresponsible."

"So what happened afterward?" I ask. "With the publicity? How did people react?"

"I'll tell you how a specific person reacted," Sam says, "and that's my boss. He fired me. Watched the footage I brought back and handed me my papers that afternoon. Said we weren't in the business of fiction. Invited me to find work elsewhere."

"But you did," I say. "History 14—right?"

"History 14 is ours," Francie says. "We created it. Which is why, as you can see, we do not live in luxury. Some viewers appreciate the additional information we bring to our broadcasts through the use of clairvoyants and other people with extraordinary abilities, and some viewers do not."

"And those viewers watch History 1," Sam says scornfully. "Where facts do not necessarily interfere with the information being broadcast."

History 1. That was the organization Bryan threatened might do the story about Jake and me if we didn't let Bryan interview us first.

"So, are the histories like the news?" I ask. "They show stuff from the past, but also current stories?"

"Yes, that's right," Sam tells me. "I suppose the rationale is that everything, once it's happened, is history—right? It's just a name that stuck."

"So what do you guys do that's different from the others?" I ask. "I mean, how do you use the psychics?"

"That's how I believe we can help you," Francie says. "I have one particular person in mind. I'm going to contact her now, and see if she can come into the studio this afternoon. I think you'd be very interested in meeting her."

"It's why I suggested you speak to my parents," Daniel says. "I knew they had resources."

"I can't guarantee anything," Francie tells me. "These are human beings—they're not machines. Some days are better than others for them. Sometimes their sight is clear, sometimes not so clear.

"But I'm going to ask one of our most reliable participants. She's a specialist at flesh sight."

"Flesh sight?" I ask.

"Touching human remains," Francie says, "and seeing that person's life, and death. I think in your situation, she's exactly what we need."

While Daniel's mother goes into another room to place the comm call, and Daniel's father calls the studio to arrange for a recording room, Daniel and I stay where we are in the kitchen.

"Why didn't you ever tell me any of this?" I ask him. "We spent all that time together in the Alps, and you never said a word. You just let me babble on about myself all the time."

Daniel shrugs. "Habit, I suppose. Self-preservation. One becomes accustomed to hiding certain facts."

"But why?" I ask. "Didn't you think I'd be interested? I would have loved to hear about all of it."

Daniel looks me in the eye. "I wanted to impress you. I wasn't certain having mad parents would accomplish that."

"They're not mad," I say quietly. "I think they're

great. I think what they're doing is really bold and exciting."

"Sarah thinks so, too," he says. "She's never been shy about talking them up. Of course, she's shy about very little. I'm certain if we'd all spent more time together in the mountains, she would have told you about them eventually."

"Thank you for the idea of telling your parents," I say, reaching over and giving his hand a squeeze. "Maybe they really can help."

Daniel moves his hand away. "Right. Shall we go then?"

43

History 14 has a studio in a building that looks a lot smaller from the outside than it actually is inside. Maybe that's because it's squished between a bakery on one side and a bike repair shop on the other.

"Not the grandest of addresses," Francie tells me as we go inside, "but well within our budget for the past twenty years."

I hear a few whispers of "Halli Markham" as Daniel and his parents and I make our way past the staff and up the stairs.

"Not many celebrities on a daily basis," Sam explains. "We mostly work with people no one has heard of. And they usually prefer us to keep it that way."

"Many of them don't even want to be paid," Francie says. "Which also works well for our budget."

"Why don't they want to be paid?" I ask.

"Dilutes the skill, for some of them," she says. "Others view it as humanitarian work—they don't want to sully it by charging money. So they come in here, put their talents to use, then go back to their regular jobs.

"Like Olga, whom you'll be meeting," Francie says. "She and her daughter own a flower shop round the corner. Olga heard word of what we were doing, and showed up one day, ready to use her abilities however we needed her."

We reach the second floor and walk down a narrow hallway. Daniel's father opens one of the doors and ushers us inside.

It's another deceptively large room. From the hallway you'd never know that where we're standing now is almost as big as the guest room where I stayed at Halli's parents' house.

It's divided into two areas: a control room, where we are now, filled with all sorts of monitors and equipment, and a smaller recording area in front of us, separated from the control room by a clear, see-through wall.

There's a technician in the control room, already setting up for the session.

"This is Julius," Sam tells me. "Julius, Halli Markham."

That gets his attention. He looks up from the

controls, smiles and turns a little red, then wipes his hand off on his pants before offering it to me.

"You can trust him," Francie tells me. "He's one of us."

I'm not exactly sure what that means—"one of us"—but I nod just the same.

"Why don't you give her a quick preview?" Sam asks Julius.

"Right," he says, then clears his throat a couple of times. "Right. Well, this area over here is for playback . . ." And he goes on to describe the process. I'm sure from the way he's describing it he expects me to understand some of the technology, so I just keep nodding and acting like I get it. And I do get some of it, just not all.

A voice comes into the control room. "Mrs. Kopeck is here."

"I'll go," Sam says, then he leaves the room.

I'm not sure what to expect. I've never met a psychic before. I wonder if she'll be dressed like a fortune teller, with a long black dress and a fringed red shawl, and have long, bushy black hair.

But as Sam brings her into the recording area I see she just looks like a normal person. Like someone's grandma. She's dressed in high-waisted gray pants, gray shoes, and a bright coral blouse. Her hair is a curly white. She's wearing pink blush and lipstick that matches her blouse.

Sam helps her get settled into the comfortable-looking chair in the middle of the room. He says a few words to her that we can't hear. Then he goes to a box resting against the wall, and removes an object covered in cloth. He brings it to Olga, says something else, then leaves the room out a side door. He reappears in the control room a moment later.

Francie nods to Julius, who presses something on his control panel.

"Ready, Olga?" Francie asks her. "Everything all right?"

Olga nods and smiles, then settles into the chair a little deeper. She closes her eyes. And unwraps the object.

I can't exactly see what the object is. It's small enough for Olga to cup within her hands, and from here it looks dark brown and hard, like a piece of wood or a stone carving.

She rolls it back and forth between her palms for a little while, keeping her eyes closed the whole time. Sometimes she tilts her head this way or that, like she's trying to see something or listen to something a little more clearly.

Then finally she speaks.

"It's a girl," Olga says. "Seven years old. Brown hair, brown skin."

She has a slight accent—maybe Czech or Polish or something like that.

The technician adjusts some controls. In a space over to our left, a cloud of colors starts to take form.

"She is barefoot," Olga says. "Long tan dress. No belt. A red band around her wrist. No, not a band—markings. Into her skin, showing ownership. She is a slave."

The cloud to our left molds itself into the girl. With all the features Olga is describing.

"She is . . . Persian," Olga says, squinting her closed eyes. "Blue edging on the top of her dress. She is carrying a bag of something . . ."

Olga is silent, her head tilted to the side as she listens or watches or however she's doing it.

But meanwhile the cloud is working on its own, becoming clearer and better-defined at every moment. Now we can see the bag. A marketplace. Other people.

"Yes, dead at seven," Olga says. "Buried with her mistress. Mistress is Scythian, not Persian. Died of lungs—bad lungs. Girl is named Nefiri. She is taking the bag to her mistress. It is herbs, they will not work, the woman dies."

The cloud focuses on the girl, walking in the middle of this busy marketplace, surrounded by merchants' stalls. There are other children, too, about her same age, but we can't see their faces—they look fuzzed out. Just vague outlines of other people around her, with Nefiri the clearest image of all.

"She knows her mistress is sick," Olga says. "She knows if the mistress dies, she will die, too."

I study the girl's expression: is she sad? Scared? Worried? She just looks . . . busy. Like she's working. Like it's just a typical errand.

"Go to the burial," Francie tells her. "How are they laid out?"

The cloud swirls again, resets. Now the background is dark. No more people or color around her. Just Nefiri, lying on her back, eyes open, looking around.

"Hands bound," Olga says. "Tied together, then tied to one of her mistress's wrists."

Sam whispers something to his wife. Francie asks Olga, "What is the mistress wearing? And age?"

Olga tilts her head and squints. "Twenty, twenty-one. Tall, but small feet. Pale skin, hair grayish-white. Like ash."

We all watch the cloud as it forms itself into the ash-haired woman.

"Dress?" Francie asks.

"Brick red. Dusty. Dirty. Oh, yes, I see." Olga is nodding to herself. "All in ash. Her hair has been painted with it, the clothes dusted with it. Her face, too. Ash base, stripes wiped away in a pattern. Like this."

Olga demonstrates by wiping two fingers down one of her cheeks. "Both sides," she says. "And here." She passes a finger under her eye. "Just on the left side."

The dead woman takes on exactly those markings. It's like I'm watching someone's dream come into life.

I reach over and take Daniel's hand. I can't help it. This is the most extraordinary thing I've seen, and I've seen a lot by now. He gives my hand a single squeeze, then lets go.

"Anything else?" Francie asks. "Jewelry, pottery—any artifacts?"

Olga waits and scans whatever's behind her eyes. "No," she says, "nothing."

"The feeling?" Francie asks. "Of the little girl?"

"Fear," Olga says. "Resignation. Sadness. Nefiri has a little brother she loves. She is not sure what will happen to him now. She helped take care of him."

I see the young girl's face take on exactly the expression described. I wouldn't have known how to break it down into those three elements—fear, resignation, sadness—but seeing the girl's face now, I know that's exactly what she feels.

And now I understand what's going on: The girl is alive. Her mistress is dead, and the slave girl is about to be buried alive beside her.

"Open or covered?" Francie asks.

"Open," Olga says.

"Dirt?"

"Dirt and ash," Olga says.

The cloud now shows both the girl and her mistress

together. With heaps of dirt and ash beginning to bury them.

Nefiri is brave about it, lying perfectly still, right up until the first pile covers her face. It must be a natural physical reaction to turn your head to the side, to try to spit the dirt out, to try to keep on breathing. But soon there's too much, it's too heavy, and though the girl struggles, now she's buried too deep to ever pull herself out.

I start to cry out, and quickly cover my mouth.

"Year?" Francie asks.

"Three eighty-six," Olga says. "B.C."

The cloud starts breaking up again, losing its form.

I look away. I feel sick inside. That poor, poor girl.

I hear Olga say, "Oh, this is a foot?" I look up and see her gazing at the object in her hand.

"Yes," Francie says. "That's right. Petrified. Turned into stone."

"Poor girl," Olga says, as if she read my thoughts. "Nothing she could do." She gazes at the foot for a moment more, then closes it again between her cupped hands, like she's protecting it, or keeping it warm.

"Thank you, Olga," Francie says. "That was lovely."

Olga smiles and starts to get up from her chair. "See you Thursday."

"Wait," Francie says, looking over at me. She motions for me to come forward. "We have a friend in here, Olga. We'd like you to meet her."

I'm suddenly very, very nervous. Like sweaty, and a little faint. Now that I've seen what Olga can do, I'm not sure at all that I still want to go through with this.

But Daniel gives me a nudge. Makes me move up into the center of the room where Olga can see me better.

"Hello," she says.

"Hello," I say back.

"This is our friend Halli Markham," Francie says. "Perhaps you've heard of her."

Olga considers for a moment. "No, sorry."

"She'd like to meet you," Francie says.

"All right," Olga answers pleasantly. "Send her in."

Now it's Francie's turn to nudge me in the back, to send me toward the door in the side of the control room. I'm sweating so much now I can feel it pooling underneath my armpits. For all I know I'm dripping onto the floor.

My voice is shaking. "I can't," I tell Francie. "I'm too afraid."

"Audie," she says gently, "after everything you've been through, I can't believe you're afraid of anything anymore."

"Believe it," I say. My teeth are chattering. I'm cold and shaking from the sweat.

Francie looks over at her son. Daniel steps up close to me and puts his arm around my shoulders. "Come on," he says. "I'll go in with you."

All this time Olga has been sitting there, patiently waiting for this strange girl who's freaking out over having to meet her. Maybe she's used to that. Maybe people have treated her that way her whole life.

Daniel guides me out of the control room, and then to the next door over, leading into the recording booth. As we walk in Olga gets up from her chair, takes a few steps toward me, and reaches out for my hand. I can't lift my own. Daniel has to lift it for me.

And as soon as my hand is in Olga's, her expression immediately changes. First a complete blankness that lasts a couple of seconds, and then a slowly-growing smile.

She closes her eyes and keeps hold of my hand.

"You have given me a puzzle," she says to me. "How exciting. Thank you."

She keeps a tight grip on me. I stand there, shaking, as Daniel lets go of me to go help Olga sit down again. The three of us move together. Olga's eyes are still closed. Mine are freakishly wide open.

"A double puzzle," Olga says. "One layer over another. This girl—" She tilts her head to the side, and even though her eyes are closed, it seems like she's staring right at me. "—and another. Halli? You are not Halli."

I think I'm going to throw up.

"This . . ." She lifts my hand up and down a few times. "This is Halli."

Olga opens her eyes. And she presses her finger right into my chest.

"This," she says, "is not."

44

"I . . . I think I need to sit down," I say to Daniel, but my legs are already giving way. He gets to me quickly, scoops me up, stands me back on my feet.

I see him gesture toward the control room, but his father is already racing through the door, carrying a chair. They both help lower me into it. I'm sweating and shaking, and yet Olga still hasn't let go of my hand.

Sam motions for Daniel to follow him back to the other room.

"No," I say, "please." I reach out my free hand, and Daniel takes it. Right now he's the only thing keeping me anchored in this room. I feel like I could disappear into a puddle of sweat, and just evaporate out through the ceiling. I need to feel solid. I need to feel real. Right now I feel like a ghost.

Sam closes the three of us back in and returns to the control room. Olga is still sitting placidly unconcerned, just holding onto my hand and watching whatever she's seeing behind her eyelids.

"You are in the mountains," she says. "Him," she points blindly toward Daniel, "you," she points to me, "and another you. And other people." Olga waves her hand, as if they're unimportant right now. "Cold," she says. "Snowing. A dog."

Red is in the control room with Daniel's parents, being very good right now. Maybe it's because he can still see me. He doesn't feel abandoned.

"And then . . ." Olga keeps a hold of me with one hand, and raises her other to the side of her forehead. She massages her thumb into her temple. She looks troubled.

I'm not saying a word. I'm not asking her anything, I'm not giving her any hints, I'm just sitting here trying not to pass out. My head is buzzing. I see little colored spots in front of my eyes. Daniel's hand is dry and warm against mine. He must think mine feels clammy and disgusting.

"I do not understand," she mutters to herself. Her eyes pop open. "Do you understand?" she asks me.

I shake my head no. This whole thing is a nightmare.

Olga closes her eyes once more. The room is so silent right now I don't know if any of us are breathing.

Then suddenly Olga squeezes my hand hard. "Yes! I see! Both of you! There you are!"

She swoops her free hand through the air. "One this way, the other that way. This one . . ."

And then she falls silent again. We were on such a roll! And now she's blocked again?

I have to use my voice. It sounds mechanical and far away. "This one . . . what, Olga? Please?"

She smiles and hums to herself, and swings my hand lightly back and forth. She's bonkers. She's lost it. Whatever she saw has obviously blown a circuit in her brain, and now she's just going to hum and speak gibberish for the rest of her life.

I've ruined her. I broke her.

"Alive," she says. "Alive!" She points her finger in front of her, at something over my shoulder. "Alive! She is there! I can see her!"

"Alive?" I say. "Now? She's alive now?"

"Yes!" Olga shouts. "Go to her!"

"Go to her?" I shout back. "Where?"

"There! There!" Olga keeps pointing. I look over my shoulder, but I can't see it.

But I do see Sam and Julius and Francie all waving to me frantically from the other room. They're smiling and shouting and pointing to where I know the cloud is inside that room.

"Thank you," I tell Olga. I lean forward and kiss her

on the cheek. "Thank you—you don't know how much you've helped me."

Then I pry my hand loose and shout, "Come on!" to Daniel, and race into the other room.

45

The cloud is nothing. Just a swirling gray. My heart sinks into my stomach.

"Just wait," Francie tells me, seeing my face. "We'll play it back. Julius, hurry! This girl is about to explode!"

Julius pokes and prods his control screen, and I just keep staring at the cloud. It's taking forever. I look over at Daniel. He smiles at me—a real, genuine smile. I've been waiting a long time for that, too.

Then finally the cloud takes shape again. And plays the movie that was inside Olga's head.

Starting with Daniel and me kissing.

Yeah, that's comfortable for Daniel and me to watch together right now, especially with his parents in the room.

I steal a glance sideways at him, but he actually

seems fine. He's got his arms crossed over his chest and he's just watching. Like he's curious what happens next.

I know what happens next. I recognize the moment. It's our last kiss before Daniel has to leave me. The rest of the group is there—Halli, Sarah, Martin—and the snow is just starting to come down. Red has a thin dusting of it on his back. We're all saying goodbye.

Sarah and Martin head off first, leaving Daniel and Halli and me for a few moments alone. I know what we're talking about: Halli is telling Daniel to take care of his injured ankle and be cautious hiking out. Daniel is telling us he hopes he'll see us again in a few weeks at his father's birthday party. Halli says she isn't sure because she has some business to attend to first—business I now know was that board meeting with her parents.

Daniel looks at me and he doesn't even need to say it—I can read it in his eyes. He's saying, "Try."

And I see it on my face, too: How much I want to. How sorry I am to see him go.

"Wow," I say, as much to myself as Daniel. "It's weird to see that again, huh?"

"It's nice," he says. "It must be strange for you to see yourself again after nearly a week of not seeing that in the mirror."

He's right. I hadn't thought of it that way, but he's right.

Now Olga's story of us skips forward, just like it did

with the slave girl. Halli and I are walking back to the hut, and I can see that guy Karl, the handsome German pilot, waiting for her in the distance.

I'm grateful there's no sound, because I know very well what she and I talking about right now: whether she thinks Daniel really likes me. She says he does. I tell her I hope so.

I sneak another glance at Daniel. I hope he can't read lips.

Halli and I hug. She's going off with Karl now to hike for a few more days in the Alps. Which is why they'll both still be up there three days later when the blizzard hits, and the avalanche sweeps down the mountain to kill them.

I hope I don't have to watch that. Not again. I've replayed it enough times in my mind. I remember every last second of Halli's life. It's not like I need to be reminded.

"Watch," Francie tells me. She points at the cloud. "It's just about to—there."

The cloud shivers. The holographic movie breaks up.

The colors get all swirly again, and I can't see anything for a moment. Then the cloud starts creating a new form. It splits into two. Now there are two separate clouds, still connected at their base. And each cloud starts showing a different scene.

My eyes flick between the two of them, trying to take them both in.

"Play them one by one," Francie instructs Julius. "Make it easier on her."

46

I wasn't there for any of this: Halli, sitting on the porch of the hut, tightening up her boot laces. Karl standing nearby, waiting. He's wearing his pack and looks ready to go.

But Halli doesn't. She pauses for a moment and looks out at the snow.

She says something to Karl, and he looks up at the sky. Snowflakes fall against his face. I notice that Red's coat looks whiter than it was before. The snow must be coming down harder.

Halli looks off toward the distance now, in the direction I know Daniel and the others just went.

Halli hesitates for a moment more, then rises to her feet.

She goes to Karl and hugs him. No, not just hugs

him—she grips him by the shoulders, pulls him toward her, and plants on him a far more passionate and skillful kiss than the one I just witnessed myself giving Daniel. It lasts a good long time. And it's kind of embarrassing to watch with other people in the room—especially Daniel—but I can't stop looking because I think I'm starting to realize something.

I think that technique came with this body. All this time I've thought it was because of Jake—that he was just such a superior kisser, he couldn't help but lift my own game about thirty notches.

But now I see it's more like what I experienced in the gym, working out with Ferguson. I could master all those incredibly hard feats of strength and coordination because they just came with the package. So maybe any guy kissing these lips—whether it's Karl the pilot, or Jake, or even Daniel—would have a totally different experience than if they kissed my own Audie lips.

How weird. How fascinating. How embarrassing.

"Sorry," I mutter to Daniel.

"For what?"

I'm not really sure how to answer.

Finally Halli lets go of him, smiles, says one thing more, then shoulders her pack. Then she starts sprinting across the snow, with Red running at her side.

Olga skips ahead again. And now Halli is on the trail, talking to Daniel and his group. Sarah is smiling, laughing. She throws her arms around Halli and gives her a big squeeze. Then Halli motions for her and Martin to go on, and she starts hiking along with Daniel.

"Is that what happened?" I ask. Halli's tracking information is starting to make sense.

"Yes," Daniel says. "She caught up with us and told us she was worried about the conditions. She wanted to be certain we'd get down all right."

"That was nice of her."

"She . . . said it was because she knew you'd be very sad if anything happened to us. To me . . . actually."

"Oh," I say. "Right." And I think at this moment Daniel might finally be just as uncomfortable as I am.

"In any case," Daniel says, gesturing toward the cloud, "that's how it happened. That's what I remember. Halli hiked down with us. We rode the boat together. We said goodbye at the train station—everything I told you when you first asked."

"But . . . how?" I say. "I still don't understand. I mean, I know that's what her tracking shows—and it's what you saw—but how could it all be completely different from what I saw? I know that avalanche was real—I watched her almost die. And look." I point to myself. "There's no denying I'm in here. How else could that have happened, except the way I remember it?"

"Julius?" Francie says. "Play the other one."

47

Julius shuts off cloud one, and cloud two starts to take form again.

Same beginning conversations. Same all the way to Halli and me saying goodbye to each other. I stand there watching while she and Red hike off into the distance to where I can see Karl waiting for them. It's all the way I remember it.

Then Halli and Karl hiking in the snow. It's dumping on them now, but I know it's not the day I saw —the day with the avalanche. They're walking up, not down, and to the left, not to the right. They're leaning into the wind, making progress.

Now Halli and Karl are sitting inside a hut I've never seen before, eating some sort of soup, dipping bread into the broth. Halli sits back in her chair. She smiles at Karl. I know that expression—tired, but happy. So everything is still fine.

"Watch," Francie says. As if I want to do anything else.

Now it's Halli and Red on a mountain slope. In a very familiar scene. And I was wrong—I don't want to watch at all. I know how this ends. I close my eyes and turn away.

"No," Francie says. "It's not what you think. Watch, Audie."

The blizzard is pounding them, making it impossible for them to walk. But they keep trying. Karl is a little above them, on the bend of trail just up the slope.

Then the sound. I can't hear it, but I can see it—a vibration in the ground. A low, slow rumble. Getting louder. Like sound traveling through a tunnel and finally exploding out the end.

"No, please," I say, closing my eyes again. I cover my face with my hands.

"Look!" Francie says. "Quickly."

I risk opening my eyes.

And suddenly see myself lying on my back, eyes open, staring at something above me.

I am lying on my back. Me, Audie. Me with the short hair. Me with the completely unmuscular little body. Unmistakably me.

"Oh, my—" I start out in a whisper, but then I finish by shouting, "I'm alive! Look, Daniel, it's me!"

Daniel is staring at me, too—the me in the movie— and it takes him a second longer, but then he smiles.

And now I'm shaking him by the arm. "Do you see?"

"Yes," he says, laughing, "I see." He hugs me. It feels good. I hug him back, happy to share this with someone who would care. No one else in this room knows me the way I really am. No one except Daniel would understand what it means to see that particular girl again, her face, her hair—Audie Masters, *still clearly alive.*

But then Daniel loosens his grip. "What happened?" he asks his parents.

I turn around to see what he's talking about. The image of me is gone. All that's left in my place is a featureless cloud of white.

"Where am I?" I ask. "Where'd I go?"

"I'm sorry," Sam says. "That was all."

"What do you mean, that was all?" I look into the next room. "Where's Olga? Bring her back! Ask her what else she saw!"

"That was all," Francie tells me. "We waited. She was still holding onto your hand, but nothing else came."

"But . . . she kept seeing me!" I argue. "She kept pointing and telling me to go to her. What else did she see?"

Sam shakes his head. "I'm sorry, Audie. That truly was everything."

"But she's alive, isn't she?" Daniel says. "Audie. Isn't that what this means?"

Daniel's parents exchange an uncomfortable look.

Sam is the one who answers. "When Olga told you someone was alive . . . I believe she meant Halli."

"Well, maybe," I say, "but we also saw me. I was there. That was my body at the end—tell them, Daniel."

"I'm sorry," Francie says. "I know it's confusing. We had Julius divide the two scenarios so you could view them separately, but remember, as Olga saw them, they were both unfolding at the same time."

"But . . ."

But now the truth is sinking in. I don't want it to—I want it to keep floating on top. I want to be able to skim it off and throw it away.

"You see," Sam says, "Olga watched Halli die in one scenario—"

"And live in the other," I finish for him. "Both at the same time. And that's why she was so excited."

I move away from the group of us clustered in front of the cloud, and take a few paces on my own. I have to think. None of this is clear.

"But we saw her," Daniel still wants to argue. "We saw Audie. Now. Alive."

"I think it was an artifact," his mother tells him. "Some imprint of the girl who now inhabits Halli Markham's body."

Before Daniel or I can say any more, Francie signals

to Julius. "Play back the second one. Reverse to just before the avalanche. Now, Audie, watch."

It was the part where I had my hands over my face. The part I didn't want to see. The avalanche is rumbling. Halli looks up. She throws herself over Red to protect him—

And the cloud turns white. No transition, no swirling or confusion of lights, but just cold, stark white.

And then me. Lying on my back, eyes open. Then the white again.

"I don't understand," I say. "What does that mean?"

"Play her the earlier film," Francie tells Julius. "The one of the slave girl. Just the ending."

It takes a moment, but then the cloud reforms, showing me the end of the burial of Nefiri. I have the same reaction as the first time—poor, poor girl.

But this time I don't look away. I watch it until the end.

I watch until the cloud turns white.

The room is silent. We all just stare at the cloud.

And then finally I find my voice.

"You're telling me I'm dead."

48

Daniel isn't willing to accept it yet.

"Have you ever seen that before?" he asks his parents. "That splitting? Has Olga ever seen two versions before?"

"Never," Sam says.

"She called it a puzzle," Daniel says. "A double puzzle. One layer over another. What did that mean?"

Maybe I'm more practical than Daniel, maybe I just know when something is over. When I've reached a dead end. Literally.

"It means just what she saw," I say. "One part of Halli went one way, one went the other. She died in one life and now I'm in her body. In the other life she hiked down with you and lived."

"But then where is that girl?" Daniel says, his voice

rising in intensity. "You are that girl, Audie. You are wearing the body that produced the tracking information that complies with what I saw. You are the girl I hiked down with that day. There was no other. You are the physical proof."

My head is beginning to hurt. I'm all for a deep, intellectual conversation, but this whole experience since I woke up this morning has been too emotional. I need a break. I need to go somewhere quiet and just sit in the dark and recover.

Daniel pulls out his tablet. "Look." He pokes it into life, makes a few sweeps with his finger, and finally brings up a kind of blank slate in 3-D. A sort of holographic chalkboard he can write on.

"You, Audie, are here. Right in this room. In what we'll call Body A."

He writes "Body A" on his tablet, and it shows up on the chalkboard.

"Halli—Body B," he writes, "continued onward with Karl. The tracking information for that body disappears from that moment forward. There's absolutely no record of Halli being anywhere but with Sarah and Martin and me. No record of her staying in that hut where we saw her and Karl dining, no record of her being in any avalanche."

"Okay," I say, "that's all true—but so what? What does that prove? Olga saw the avalanche, just like I did. And she saw Halli die, right? Isn't that what the white light means? So that has to be Body B, since it's the one that kept hiking."

But now I see the inconsistency. "But if Body B is the one I saw in the avalanche," I say, "then that's the one I saved—that's the one I'm in. But the tracking information doesn't show any of that. It only shows what happened to Body A."

"Precisely," Daniel says.

"So which body am I in—Body A or Body B?"

It's beginning to look suspiciously like a math problem. My brain doesn't like that one bit.

"And there's another," Daniel says. "Body C. Your body, Audie—your real one. We saw it there at the end, so where did it go?"

"Dead, isn't it?" I say, wishing I didn't have to. "Isn't that what the white light meant?"

"But how can you be sure?" Daniel asks.

"I can only tell you how Olga's vision normally works," Francie says. "When she comes to the end of a life, the image turns to white. We've seen it every single time, for as long as she's been coming here."

"But Olga said she was alive," Daniel answers. "She said to go to her. I can't believe she was only speaking of the other Halli. That wouldn't make sense—Olga knew very well that one Halli had died, the other lived. She was sitting across from the live Halli at just that moment. The only surprise was that last image of Audie. I'm certain of it."

I study the expression on Daniel's face right now: intense, serious, but also energized and almost . . . happy. He has more hope than I do in this moment. But I'm willing to let some of that hope leak onto me. Right now I could use some.

Because if Daniel's parents are right, it's all over. Whether I'm in Body A or Body B, all the other bodies are gone. White light dead and gone—including my own.

Which means I'm stuck. Permanently and irrevocably stuck in this body and this life. My former home —the girl known as Audie, the shell known as Body C— is gone. Like the traveler to another planet who comes home to find his own planet destroyed.

But I don't even have time to process that, or to feel sad, because Daniel isn't going to let me.

"Where's Olga?" he asks his parents. "Can we bring her back in here? To clarify?"

"I'm afraid it won't make any difference," Sam tells him. "Once the cloud turns white, Olga never has any information beyond that. We've tried with her before. She's told us she can't see what isn't there any longer. Her vision ends with the end of a life."

"I don't accept that," Daniel says. "I'm sorry, but I think you're wrong. Come on, Audie."

"Wait—where?"

Daniel grabs my hand. "We're going to talk to Olga."

49

I was expecting a little flower shop like the one near our grocery store at home—a kind of one-room space filled with shelves of vases, and a refrigerated case in the back for the bouquets that need to be kept cold.

But this place. Wow.

It's like the store equivalent of Halli's greenhouse: a huge, two-story space with plants and flowers *every-where*, like they've taken over the earth and if we humans don't keep moving, we'll all be swallowed by vegetation.

I hesitate inside the front door, just trying to take it all in. But Daniel is impatient.

"Come on," he says, taking my hand and leading me through a narrow tunnel of vines and yellow blossoms. It's like going through the tunnel of a cave, where you think it's always going to be that close and confined, and then suddenly you step out into this huge, wide-open space, where there might be an underground lake and thousands of stalactites hanging from the ceiling and stalagmites pushing up from the floor.

But instead here there are customers—lots and lots of customers. People milling about, browsing, sniffing, chatting, but it isn't noisy in here, which is weird. It's like the plants all sort of absorb and muffle the sound. It's really very pleasant.

And it doesn't smell. It's not at all like Halli's parents' flat, with that sickening, overpowering stench. Even though there are hundreds—probably even thousands—of roses and other kinds of flowers in here, the whole place just smells clean and damp and fresh.

I give a nervous look to Red. I remember that grad student of Professor Whitfield's, Hannah Trong, saying plants sometimes have stress reactions around dogs, but I don't know what else to do—I can't leave him outside. I hope Olga doesn't mind that I brought him in. I certainly don't see any other dogs in here.

"There she is," Daniel says, pulling me onward.

We can see Olga standing behind a counter, talking to a couple at the front of a long line. Everyone in line is holding in their arms or pushing along on a cart at least two matching plants of some sort—pairs of potted daisies and violets, and all sorts of flowers I'd never be able to name.

I hear someone whisper too loudly to her friend, "Look! It's Halli Markham."

Heads turn my way.

"And look!" the young woman tells her friend. "There's her dog, too."

"Forget the dog," her friend murmurs. "Who's that gorgeous specimen with her?"

I don't think Daniel overheard that. Which is probably fine—somehow I don't think he wants some strange girl calling him a specimen, gorgeous or not. It just doesn't seem like it's his style.

Jake, sure. But not Daniel.

Olga notices us now, too, gives a little wave, then turns her attention back to the man and woman she was talking to. Daniel pulls me closer to the front—not like we're trying to take cuts in line, but off to the side in a way that lets Olga know we're waiting for her.

"We tried him with Magda," Olga is telling the couple, "but I think Trudy is a better match. They have been together two weeks now. You see if they are happy."

The woman in the couple asks a question I can't hear, and Olga answers, "Not too much water. Siegfried prefers to be dry. Feed it to Trudy, and she can pass it along."

The man and the woman thank Olga, and leave, all smiles.

"Next?" Olga says to the next person in line.

Daniel darts forward. "Sorry," he tells the woman who's just stepped up holding what look like two miniature pomegranate trees. "Just a quick word. Mrs. Kopeck, if my friend and I could speak to you—"

Olga stares at Daniel placidly for a moment, like she's forgotten who he is. Then she surveys the line of people in front of her. "Twenty minutes," she tells us, then motions for the pomegranate woman to come forward.

"Thank you," Daniel says.

The two of us step away, and finally Daniel lets go of my hand. I notice his has been starting to sweat.

"What makes you think she'll be able to tell us anything else?" I ask, following him now past rows and rows of potted plants, toward what looks like a sitting area in back. "You heard what your parents said."

"I heard," he says. "But I'm not giving up."

"Why?" I ask. "I mean, I appreciate it—obviously—I hope you know that. It's just that . . . well, you're sort of acting . . . I just wondered why, all of the sudden?"

Now I feel stupid. Maybe I shouldn't have drawn attention to it. But it does seem odd that ever since that session with Olga, he's been acting a lot more motivated than he ever was when I was telling him my story last night, and when we were talking to his parents this morning.

Daniel stops and faces me. "You really don't know?"

"Forget it," I say. "Never mind."

Daniel looks around us, then draws me off to the side. Past rows of geraniums and snapdragons and signs that say asters and gladioli.

"I saw you," he tells me. "The real you. Do you think I can forget that?"

I think of the images formed within the cloud: Daniel and me kissing, the look that passed between us when we finally had to say goodbye. I can see how that might make him nostalgic. I can't pretend it didn't have an effect on me, either.

But it seems so long ago. Another life. I've been dealing with so much since last week, that other life—that other girl—both seem so far away.

But obviously not to Daniel. For him, that memory must be fresh. And seeing it played out again in front of us—

"I know," I tell him. "It must be really weird for you."

"No, it was nice," he says, looking at me straight in the eyes. "I miss you, Audie. I don't think you know how much."

My tongue feels dry. It's the first time Daniel has really said something personal to me. Personal like that. It's like he's been maintaining this respectful distance, careful not to say anything that might make either of us uncomfortable—except for a few questions about Jake in the beginning, but even those stopped last night. And now I've pushed Daniel back into it by asking one too many questions.

"I . . . I've missed you, too," I answer him. And I know it's true. I like Daniel—I always have, ever since I first met him. Nothing has happened to change that. It's just that Jake has sort of moved in and taken over the spot, and pushed Daniel out to the sides where he barely has any room. It's not Daniel's fault—he hasn't done anything to deserve it—it's just what's happened because of things beyond either of our control.

"I can't accept this," Daniel tells me quietly. "I know it's you in there, but who you are right now . . . everything I've seen . . ."

Daniel shakes his head and looks off to the side. Like he's not sure whether he should say any more.

I reach out my hand to him, but he doesn't take it.

"The truth is," he says, "you're not the girl I'm in love with. And I'm willing to do anything to get her back."

50

"Here you are," Olga says.

There's no way twenty minutes have gone by. Or maybe an hour has gone by. I'm sort of standing here stunned at the moment, trying to sort out how I feel about what Daniel just said.

"I asked Bethany to cover the line," Olga tells us. "Let us go through here."

She points down an aisle of miniature lemon and orange trees, back to where I think Daniel had been leading me before.

The two of us walk along silently behind Olga. I can't look at Daniel right now. There's a thick current of some kind of energy passing between us, and it's making my face hot and the rest of my skin feel clammy.

There's a whole second shop, it looks like, behind the flower store. A café. The sign above the doorway says, "No tablets or other devices, please."

The place is quiet. Soft. Soft lighting, soft sounds. There are people sitting at tables, and they're either talking quietly or reading books.

Books. Paper books. Just like Daniel was reading last night. It seems so primitive and so welcome to my eyes.

"Cricket?" Olga calls to a woman behind the counter. She's just dishing out a huge slice of some sort of sumptuous cake to a man who looks worried now that Olga might interrupt that process.

But the woman smiles at him and finishes their transaction so the man can go off to a corner table and enjoy his selection in peace.

"This is my daughter," Olga says, "Cricket."

"Christine Kopeck," the woman says. She has Olga's blue eyes and pale, pleasant features, and dark blond hair instead of white. And she sounds British, instead of whatever Olga is.

Daniel offers her his hand, but Christine simply nods to both of us and keeps her hands at her sides.

"Can you speak to these two young people for a moment?" Olga asks her daughter. "Privately."

Christine's smile fades. Clearly she isn't happy with the request.

"They will not stay long," Olga tells her. "You know I do not normally ask."

Christine bites the inside of her lip and looks from Daniel to me. Then finally she nods. She takes off her apron, whispers something to one of her workers, then motions for the three of us to follow her into the back.

"But," Daniel says to Olga, "I'm sorry, I don't mean to be rude, but we were hoping to speak to you, Mrs. Kopeck."

"I think my Cricket can be of greater use," she answers.

We enter a small office, clean and bright, with small trees and pots of flowers pushed up against the walls. Again I notice the pairings—never one particular flower without another pot just like it right next to it. Same with the trees.

I'm curious enough I ask Olga about it, even though there are obviously other matters to deal with.

"Plants get lonely, too," she says. "I would never send one away alone. They die after a place like this, leaving all their friends. Anyone who buys from me, buys two."

"What was that thing about the water?" I ask. "What you said about giving one of them—Trudy, I think— water and not any to Siegfried?"

"They will take care of each other," Olga says. "We have seen it. A dry plant is nursed by his friends."

"That's actually true," Daniel says. "I've seen it, too. In the laboratory."

Daniel has never told me anything about his studies in school. I know he's won at least one science award, but when I asked him about it before, he sort of shrugged it off. It was clear he felt shy talking to me about it, so I never pursued it any further.

And yesterday, at the café with Sarah and her friends, he seemed perfectly fine with his sister breezing right past his neurobotany thing, and moving on to other topics.

So even though this is the perfect opportunity to follow up and find out more, I decide to let it go. I've pressed him enough today. From now on if he wants to tell me something, he should do it on his own.

Just like he did a few minutes ago. Which I'm still not sure how I feel about.

I turn the conversation back to Olga.

"You name your plants?" I ask her. "Like Siegfried and Trudy?"

"Of course they have names," Olga answers. "We all have names. We are all individuals, are we not? Is your name Halli, or something else? Who do you prefer to be?"

That catches me off guard. Daniel sees it, too. He's watching me now, waiting for my answer.

"I . . . I prefer to be Audie," I say. "Halli is . . . too hard."

"Ah," Olga says. "Just so."

"Is that what this is about?" Christine asks her mother.

"It is a puzzle," Olga says. "I know only part of it. You can tell us more."

"I don't like to," Christine says.

"I know," her mother answers. "But sometimes it is a kindness. And if you can ease a person's mind, sometimes you should. This girl has a special circumstance. She needs to understand what has happened."

"And you couldn't tell her?" Christine asks.

"Only the past," Olga says. "Not her present."

Christine sighs. Heavily. She closes her eyes and presses her fingers against them.

I look at Daniel. He's watching Christine. The moments tick by, and she still sits there silently pressing her eyes.

I whisper to Olga, "Maybe we should leave."

"No," she and Daniel both say together.

"Give her time," Olga whispers. "It is not so easy for her as it is for me."

Finally Christine speaks. "Alone?" she asks her mother.

"I will come," Olga answers.

Christine gets up and moves around the side of her desk, and stands between Olga and me. Daniel positions his chair so she can sit down. Then Christine holds out a hand first to her mother, then one to me.

"Please don't say anything," Christine tells Daniel

and me. "No matter what happens. It's hard for me to concentrate."

Daniel and I both nod. The room feels so thick with energy right now, I wonder why the plants aren't bursting into flame.

Christine squeezes my hand. And off we go.

51

We are inside the cloud. Not the cloud from Francie and Sam's control room, but a cloud I remember very well. It's where I spent hours—maybe even days—after I slammed into Halli and pushed her off the mountain to try to save her life. It's where I stayed lost for who knows how long until I woke up in her house, inside her body, and had to take over living her life.

It isn't like before, with Olga. Christine isn't saying anything. All I have is the feeling to tell me when we're moving from one situation to another.

And now the feeling I have is one of warmth. Of light. Out of the cloud into colors and brightness and a kind of liquid heat.

It is liquid, I realize. I'm deep inside it somewhere,

not breathing, but not needing to breathe. I know Christine and Olga are near, but I've lost touch with them. I'm not afraid, though, because this place feels familiar. I don't feel lost the way I did before. I think I can pull myself out and find a way to the light.

Then I feel the pressure of both of them holding my hands again, and now the three of us are standing on the side of a street. A street I know very well. I look across from me and see houses that I've looked at every day since I was a little girl.

And coming out of one of those houses, pausing to tighten the lace on her sneaker before setting off on a morning jog, is a person I know so well I almost break my promise to Christine and scream out her name. She has short hair and my face, and she's just about to pass us when I let go of Olga's and Christine's hands, and leap into the running body and feel my foot landing on the asphalt with its very next step.

Halli stops. I can feel her. I can feel her thoughts and her presence and maybe this is her soul. But whatever it is, she feels mine, too, and now she's thrown her arms around us, and she's hugging herself and jumping up and down and shouting, "Audie! You're alive! You're here!" She keeps jumping and laughing and shouting, "Audie! You're alive—you're alive!"

And then Christine loses control.

And I'm ripped out of my body once more.

I am crying so hard I can't breathe. Daniel is bent over me, holding me, trying to find out if I'm all right. He thinks maybe I'm hurt. I am—I'm so hurt if I start screaming I know I'll never stop.

It's not Christine's fault. I know it's because Halli spoke. Christine lost her grip and she couldn't hold on. And now she's so upset she's shaking, and Olga is trying to comfort her. I can't say anything about what happened or I'm going to make it worse.

But to be ripped apart again, ripped out of my own body like that, sent shooting back across whatever great divide is between Halli and me—it was like having my skin torn off in one long strip, like having my hair pulled out from the roots, like having all my teeth broken to bits with a hammer. My body feels like it's on fire. Every single nerve is burning like the tip of a match.

I'm so antsy, so edgy, I need to stand up. I'm not crying any more, but I need to move. To burst through these doors and go run fifty miles. Something to use up all this excess energy.

Daniel holds me by the shoulders and searches my face. "Please," he says, "tell me. Tell me what happened."

"She's alive," I say. "We both are. Halli is in my body and we're alive. I was in there with her. We both felt it."

Daniel shouts out a laugh and then hugs me so hard he lifts me off my feet. He kisses me hard on my cheek before he sets me down.

I look past him to Christine. I don't want her to be broken. She did me a favor—I understand now how hard that was for her.

Olga is speaking to her softly in whatever language she speaks. Christine is nodding. The energy in the room is settling down—I can feel it.

But the plants nearest to me aren't doing so well. All the leaves on one of the trees are completely wilted, and one of the flowers looks like it dropped all its petals. I'm sure they didn't look that way when we came in here.

"I'm so sorry," I tell Christine. "I hope that didn't hurt you."

Her face is grave. "I felt what you felt. I'm sorry for you, too."

Daniel looks worried. "It's nothing," I tell him. "It's passed."

I sit back in my chair, and Daniel sits on the arm of it, still keeping his hold on me. I want it right now. I'm glad he's not letting go.

I wait until Olga and her daughter are done speaking in their private language, but then I finally have to ask.

"Can you explain to me what happened? How did you find her—me?"

Christine glides her hand through the air, like it's riding on a wave.

"Vibrations," she says.

And I know exactly what she means.

53

"It's why I can't have any devices in the café," Christine explains. "I can feel every vibration moving through the air in such a small space. It makes me want to jump out of my skin. I can't bear it more than a few seconds."

"The plants are good for her," Olga says. "They dampen the noise and vibration."

Christine nods.

"What did you see?" I ask Daniel.

"Nothing," he says. "The three of you held hands and closed your eyes. And then suddenly you were screaming."

No wonder he was so concerned. Seeing me disappear the few times I did was probably more relaxing.

"Christine," I say, "can you please explain to me how you did it? How did you find us?"

Because we are an "us"—Halli and me. This whole time I've been thinking of myself over here as me, alone without her. But just that brief moment back inside my body, sharing it with Halli, made me see how wrong I've been. She and I have always been together on this since we first met. Entangled. Inseparable. I've felt so alone this whole time, when obviously that wasn't possible. If I'm in her body, then of course we're still connected. And knowing she landed inside mine proves it all the more.

"It wasn't easy," Christine tells me. "I've never had to push so far."

"What do you mean?" I ask.

"I can tell you, standing behind my counter out there, what someone on the other side of the world is doing right this minute. Or whether there's someone out in the plant shop trying to take a cutting from something and sneak it out in their pocket."

"I see the past," Olga says, "my Cricket sees the present."

"But this wasn't the present," Christine tells us. "That's what felt so strange."

I don't like the sound of that. "If this wasn't the present," I say, "then when was it?"

Christine waves her hand backward over her shoulder. "Just . . . before." She turns to Olga. "Mum, do you know? You're better at time."

"Eight-twelve in the morning," she answers.

I relax. The "before" Christine was talking about is just the time difference. I'm so busy trying to do the math—I'm not really sure what time it is here, but I think England is either seven or eight hours ahead of Arizona—I almost miss what Olga says next:

"Saturday."

"Saturday?" Daniel and I both say together.

"What date?" Daniel asks.

"October thirteen," Olga answers.

Daniel shakes his head. "That was last Saturday," he says. "Three days ago. Today's the sixteenth."

"No," I say. "No, no, no—" I'm on my feet again, pacing. "That's impossible."

"More impossible than any of this?" Daniel asks me.

But I'm too busy trying to keep up with my whirring mind. Thinking back about the lost days.

At first I thought I'd only lost two—the ones between Tuesday, when I saw Halli with the avalanche, and Thursday when I woke up in her body.

But then Jake convinced me I'd actually lost four days —all the way back to the Sunday before, when Halli's tracking showed her hiking down from the mountain and going back to Munich. And I've seen that scenario for myself now, in the scenes played out in Olga's cloud.

But now Olga is talking about three days. Saturday to Tuesday, Sunday to Thursday—I feel like I've completely lost track of my own timeline, and I don't know if I'm past or present or future.

"None of this makes any sense!" I say. "Daniel, do you understand what's going on?"

"No," he says, "I don't."

I'm pressing my palms against my temples, as if that will help. Christine gives me a sympathetic look.

"I don't like it either," she says. "I never like it. My mum does."

"It is because I hold it loosely," Olga says.

"Hold what loosely?" I ask.

"Time," she says. "You want it to be—" She knifes the side of one hand against the palm of another. "—everything exact. Even. One second, two second, one year, this year. But time is . . ." She makes the same rolling gesture with her hand that Christine made earlier. "Waves. Motion. We can rise above the waves and dive back in, anywhere we choose. You understand?"

"No," I tell her. "I'm sorry. I'm completely lost right now."

Olga turns to Daniel. "You understand?"

"I think . . . yes, I think I do," he says. "I'm beginning to."

"He is the right one for you," Olga tells me. "He is smart. Not that other one—the black-haired boy."

Daniel and I both look at each other with shock. And then Daniel is nice enough to laugh.

"She thinks she's a matchmaker, too," Christine says. Then she scolds her mother in their private language.

I'd love to ask her how she knows about Jake, but not in front of Daniel.

Then I realize that's part of my past, just as much as where this body went when Halli decided to hike down the mountain with Daniel and Sarah and Martin. That history was just a little further back. My history with Jake is more recent, but it's still my history—or at least the history of Body A or Body B or whoever it turns out I am. Olga must have seen it.

"So how do I get back?" I ask the two women. "How can I find Halli again?" Forget trying to figure out all the mathematics of time—right now I just need some trick. "Can you take me there again? Help me stay there longer?"

"I cannot let my Cricket do it again," Olga says. "It is too hard."

"I'm sorry," Christine agrees. "I really can't. Not right now. Maybe in a few days."

"I can't wait a few days," I tell her. "Halli is waiting for me now—I know it. If I can just find the way back—"

"You must rise above," Olga tells me. "Find the wave. Dive back in."

Oh, sure, I think. That's all.

54

The four of us emerge from Christine's office, and two things happen at once:

A man I've never seen before jumps right in front of Daniel and me and points his oversized binoculars at us and shouts, "Halli Markham! Who's the new man in your life?"

And Olga smashes her hand against the binoculars and sends them crashing to the floor.

"No devices!" she shouts at the man. "None!" She turns and waves her daughter back into the office. Then the wrath of a mother comes down hard on the man.

"Leave here! Now! Who are you? Leave!"

"History 1," the man says, scrambling to pick up his

camera. "We just want a few words with Miss Markham—"

"Get out!" Olga shouts at him, herding him out through the doorway of the café, into the plant part of the building. Daniel and I hang back, watching in amazement as this small woman completely bullies a man twice her size.

But I understand Olga's passion: she isn't protecting Daniel or me, she's protecting Christine from whatever vibrations the man's camera might be giving off.

There's a crowd gathered amongst the flowers and trees, and they aren't all customers. There are more people out there with binocular cameras to their faces, trying to catch some glimpse of Daniel and me.

Someone in the crowd must have tipped them off. I didn't even think about it at the time. Any of those customers could have seen Daniel holding my hand as we entered the store, or watched us having an obviously intense conversation off by ourselves. Then all it took was a comm call to right person, and suddenly there are all these reporters.

I scan what faces I can see, looking for Bryan. I wonder if he's out there.

I feel a hand tugging on my arm. "Come on."

It's Daniel, and Christine is tugging on him. She pulls us both back into her office and closes the door. Then she points to another door at the other end of the room.

"Go upstairs," she tells us. "It's our apartment. There's another door from there out onto the street."

"Thank you," I tell her. "I'm so sorry for all the trouble—"

"I'll help you," she says, "if you need me. Let me rest for a few days. But maybe by then you won't need my help. What I do isn't special. My mother has a gift, but I'm ordinary."

I start to protest, but Christine goes on.

"She taught me. Since I was a little girl. She showed me how to concentrate. I can see things because I open myself up to them. But I don't like to do it anymore because it makes me too sensitive to everything else. I didn't use to mind so much, but it's gotten worse over the years. But maybe you're not like that. Not everybody is. You should try."

"How?" I ask.

"Focus," Christine says. "Concentrate. You know where to go now, so open yourself up to it. Rise above the waves, like my mum said. Wait until you feel the right one, then dive down."

"You make it sound easier than it is," I say.

"It is easy," Christine says. "I could do it from when I was three. I bet either of you could do it any day. You just have to try."

"I could, too?" Daniel asks.

"Why not?" Christine answers. "I'm telling you the

truth: I'm nothing special. It's like learning to play the piano. You practice till you know the notes."

Olga sticks her head in through the door. "There are more coming." Then she says something in her own language that I'm pretty sure is a curse word.

"You should leave," Christine tells us. She opens the door leading up to their apartment. "Come back if you need me, but try not to need me. Please."

I nod. I understand. I can't believe this total stranger has done so much for me already.

I reach for her hand to shake it, but she pulls back. I understand that, too. Enough contact—and everything that comes with it—for one day.

"You remember," Olga tells me, pointing at Daniel. "This one, not the other."

Daniel gives me an amused look.

"I'll remember," I mumble, just to keep her from saying more. She's done a lot for me today, too. The least I can do in return is show her proper respect.

But I don't need matchmaking, thank you. What I need is a dark, quiet room where I can concentrate. Because Halli is waiting for me right now, I know it.

Now all I have to do is find her again.

55

The apartment looks like what you'd expect: plants everywhere, lots of windows to allow in natural light, the same kind of tamped down, muted quality to the air like in the shop downstairs, making the whole place feel completely peaceful and quiet.

I can see why Olga and Christine would want to live here. I could live in a place like this, too. It's like Halli's house in Colorado: not too much furniture, plenty of books lining the walls, rugs and pillows and other furnishings in colors that feel good on the eyes, like soft greens and muted rose.

It's tempting to just stay here. Park myself on their couch and take a break from my life. Close my eyes and see if I can find that wave Christine was describing. Just try it right here and now.

"We should go," Daniel says.

"Yeah," I say, "we should."

But we both still stand where we are for another minute. Daniel obviously likes it here, too.

"Are you all right?" Daniel asks me.

"Yeah. Why?"

"You seem . . . tired."

"I am tired," I admit. In fact, I feel slightly wrecked. "But it's fine," I say. "We're so close now. I just need to find somewhere where I can be alone so I can try to contact Halli again. Any ideas?"

"Yes, a perfect one, in fact," he says. "Come with me."

We find the door leading outside and step out into the shadows of the afternoon. Red bounds ahead of us, racing down the stairs.

I see why.

His favorite stick-thrower is here.

Daniel mutters something under his breath.

"How did he—?" But of course I know. Jake's standing there holding his tablet. He's been tracking me. He must have access through Halli's parents. It was helpful to me at one time, but now it's just irritating.

"I'm sorry," I tell Daniel. "I'll go tell him we're busy."

"Halli Markham is very popular today," he answers.

Jake is standing next to the car that dropped me off last night. That same driver is inside.

Jake and Red are having a fine reunion, with Red

leaping and spinning in place. Jake fluffs up his ears, pats his sides, generally returns the happy greeting.

As soon as Daniel and I are near, Jake straightens up. "Everett," he says.

Daniel gives him a nod.

Jake smiles at me. "Do you have a minute?"

"Uh . . . not really. We're kind of in the middle of something. Can I talk to you later tonight?"

"Just a minute," Jake says, opening the door to the car. Red hops right in.

I bend down to get him out, and see that there's someone else in the car. Bryan.

"Can I talk to you?" he says.

I look back at Daniel. He simply stands and waits, letting me make the decision for myself.

"Don't leave," I tell Daniel. "I'll be right back."

I slide in. Jake slides in after me and closes the door. It's a roomy back seat, but three people and a huge dog are pushing the limits.

"I got a call this afternoon," Bryan says. "Can you guess who from?"

"Uh . . . not really."

"My producer. Can you guess why?"

Yes, I can guess. All those reporters, and Bryan not among them.

"Your parents gave me an exclusive, Halli. Do you understand what that means?"

I don't appreciate his tone. He's speaking to me like a child. If he knew half the things I've seen—today alone.

Maybe he can tell from my face that he's going about it the wrong way, because he sighs and leans back and starts again.

"They can fire me for this, you know," he says. "I'm supposed to be with you all the time, grabbing coverage, intimate moments, the 'real Halli Markham.'"

"I'm sorry," I say. "I didn't want you to get into trouble."

"What's the story with this guy?" Bryan asks, gesturing toward Daniel standing outside. "Was I wrong about you and Jake?"

"Can we discuss all this some other time?" I say. "I have something else I need to do right now."

"*Is* there something going on?" Jake asks me. "I told Bryan no, but if you can't even answer the question—"

"There's nothing between Daniel and me. He's just a friend. But he needs help with something right now, and I promised I'd help him, so if we could just talk about all of this later—"

"When, later, Halli?" Jake says. "I don't understand what you're doing. We were supposed to be over here touring your parents' facility, and now you're doing . . . what? Going to flower shops—"

"And rival history organizations," Bryan adds.

"—and having reporters follow you and ask you questions about that guy out there—"

"And they're not going to stop," Bryan says. "We found you first right now, but it's not going to take them long to track you down. They know what Daniel looks like, and they'll find his house and his school—"

"Enough, all right! Enough!" I shout. Red wags his tail nervously. "What do you two expect me to do?"

"Your parents sent me over with you to look out for you," Jake says. "They're going to wonder why I let you get away. How's it going to look when they see you and Daniel show up on some history program tonight?"

"Exactly," Bryan says. "Your parents gave me the exclusive because they knew I'd make you—and them—look good. I can't do that if you won't let me in. Look, I was willing to give you and Jake a break last night—tell it the way you wanted it told. But now you're making it awfully hard to tell that story anymore. Not if you're out there in public flaunting it with some other guy—"

"I'm not *flaunting* anything! This is ridiculous. I don't care what my parents think or your producer thinks."

"Do you care what I think?" Jake asks.

"Yes, but not when you're wrong. I have friends here. They need my help right now. I'm going to do what I want."

I open the car door. I'm feeling very Halli all of the sudden—and very unwilling to be bossed around.

Maybe it's because I'm so close to turning this life back over to her. I don't want to deal with any of this other garbage anymore if I don't have to.

"I'll call you later," I tell Jake. "Come on, Red. We have to go."

"You're making a mistake," Bryan says.

"I make them all the time," I answer. "I'm getting really good at it by now."

I make sure Red's tail is clear, then I slam the door. And turn to Daniel.

"Apparently the other reporters aren't going to give up," I tell him. "They're going to camp outside your house until we both confess we're secretly married."

"Sarah will love the attention, I'm afraid. Even though she'll wonder how I could ever cheat on Audie with you. She won't like that one bit. Very romantic, that girl."

I press my head between my hands. If Jake is watching, he probably thinks it's my old head injury acting up. I drop my hands so he won't think he needs to whisk me away to a doctor.

"Suggestions?" I say.

"Come with me," Daniel says. "I still know a place. They may find you there, but they won't get in."

I let out a breath. "Good. Perfect. Because if this goes on much longer, I'm going to have to hit someone."

"Preferably not me," Daniel says. "You may have

noticed you're considerably stronger than you once were."

"That's right," I tell him. "And don't you forget it."

We are back at History 14, where Daniel promises me the reporters will never get past the reception desk. His parents are in on it, too, and assure me that even though a reporter might dare violate Olga and Christine's sign and try to bring a camera into the café, there's an unwritten rule among the history organizations that none of them breach each other's security. Daniel and I will be fair game once we step back out onto the street or even go back home to his house, but within the walls of the studio, we're safe.

Daniel leads me up to the third floor.

"No one is ever up here this time of day," he says. "And I'll stand watch outside just to make certain you aren't disturbed."

"Thank you, Daniel." There's a reason why I've always felt so safe with him around.

He opens the door to one of the rooms. It's small in here—maybe a quarter the size of the recording booth where Olga had her session. And there's just one piece of furniture: a black mound on the floor that sort of looks like a bean bag chair.

I sit down and sink into it. There aren't beans in there, but some sort of gel instead that molds itself around me and makes me feel almost weightless. It's like floating in a bubble bath, without the wet.

Red stretches out on the floor beside me.

"Do you need anything else?" Daniel asks, his hand already on the door to leave.

"Yes," I tell him. I didn't know I was going to ask him before this moment, but now I realize I'm right. "I'd really like you to stay in here with me. I think it would help."

Daniel hesitates. "But won't that interfere?"

"I don't think so. And to tell you the truth, I don't really want to do it by myself. I don't think it will work."

"Why wouldn't it work?"

"I don't know, I just . . . it's just a feeling." And it's one of those things you don't realize is true until you hear yourself saying it out loud. "You're part of this, Daniel. You were there when Olga and Christine and I found her, and I think you should be here now. And I know you won't say anything or try to ruin my concentration—you're not like other people." Like Jake, for instance, who would see it as the perfect opportunity to make out with me. "Just . . . sit with me, Daniel. Please. Trust me on this."

He hesitates a moment more, then gives in. I make room for him on the chair. It takes a little maneuvering until the gel conforms itself to our new shape. But even now, even with us so close, I can tell Daniel is trying to keep some space between us.

"You can touch me, you know," I tell him. "It's not like I'm not used to you. Come closer—I don't care." I pull his sleeve toward me and make him settle in more comfortably. Then I lean my head against his shoulder.

And it's what I want right now. Just something—someone—cozy and safe and kind. Someone to protect me. Not someone who's going to gang up on me with some reporter and try to get me do something I don't want to when I've already said I'm busy and need to call him later, but Jake never wants to take no for an answer—

"Audie?" Daniel asks. "Are you all right?"

I've got my hand over my eyes, trying to block out my life. But that's not going to work. I need to go find my other life first, then I can give Halli this one back.

I reach down and grab onto Daniel's hand. I've gotten used to that lately, in times of stress. I like the feel of it—the warmth and solidity of it—and right now it feels like the right thing.

But not for Daniel, apparently. He pulls his hand away.

"What is wrong with you?" I ask him. "Why don't you like me anymore?"

"Like you?" Daniel twists himself sideways so he can look at me. "Audie, I love you—I thought I made that clear. But you are not Audie right now. I'm sorry, but I don't feel right being . . . intimate toward you. Not when you're like this."

I can't help it. I have to laugh. "You mean you think you're cheating on me? With me?"

"You may be accustomed to wearing that body," he says, "but I can't be. You're Halli. I want Audie. So please go and find her."

Now I'm not laughing. Because I understand what he means.

"So you just want the way I look," I say. "It doesn't matter that this really is me inside."

"No, I want the way you *were*," Daniel says. "With me. Not with Jake or anyone else." He starts to get out of the chair. "I should go. This can't be any help to you—"

I pull him back into the gel. "Don't go. Please. Just . . . stay."

We both lie back again and let the gel re-enfold us.

I turn on my side so I can look at him. "I understand," I say. "And I'm sorry. I know it must be hard for you. But please—" I reach down and take his hand again and lift it up between us. "You and I are in this together now. We're the only ones. So please—at least be my friend."

"Of course I'm your friend," he says. "I'm always your friend."

"You promise?" I ask.

"Audie," Daniel says. "Come here."

He pulls his hand away again, but this time it's so he can slip it underneath my back. Then he brings me closer, lets me curl my knees up, rest my head on his chest and fit myself against him. Like he's another feature of this chair, holding me and surrounding me in his warmth and comfort.

He kisses the top of my head.

"Will that do?" he asks quietly.

"Yes. Thank you," I whisper back. And I know it's wrong, but I wish so much he would kiss me right now on the lips. But I know that's not possible. Daniel has too much integrity. Which makes me wish even more that he would kiss me.

But we're not here for that. We're here to get me back. Then that girl is the one who can reclaim her boyfriend.

So I close my eyes. I breathe deeply.

And begin searching for Halli's wave.

57

It's an interesting thing, to forget about time, and instead try to view it like an ocean. To see it in ripples and whitecaps, imagine a decade over there, a century over here, today in this one splash, last week just an arm's length away.

But that's how I coax my brain to see it. To stop thinking in linear terms, but instead look at all of time as a whole.

I imagine myself floating above it, like a sea gull riding the air. My wings outstretched, giving a flap or two to hold my position, but just relaxing here and taking it all in.

And I wait for the feeling. That same feeling I had before, when Christine and Olga and I held hands. This time it's Daniel I feel breathing beside me, but it's really the same thing. Maybe what Christine said is right, and she isn't special, and anyone can do this. We just have to learn to concentrate. To find our anchors here in the real world and meanwhile let our minds journey free.

I slip back into the liquid. Where it's pointless to open my eyes, because there's nothing to see. And pointless to breathe, because I don't need to. This is an in-between place, a holding place, and what I remember is what it felt like to come out of it, back onto my street at home. I just have to wait for that moment again, don't push it, just wait and let it tell me—

"Heya," Halli says inside my head.

"Heya," I say inside of hers.

5 8

She is sitting on the curb. The same curb where Christine and Olga and I stood hours ago.

"I was afraid to leave," Halli tells me. "I was afraid you couldn't find me again. But you're here!"

Anyone watching right now will see a young woman hugging herself and laughing and bouncing up and down. And I don't care. Halli doesn't care, either. Caring is for people with boring, ordinary lives.

"Is Red all right?" Halli asks. "Please tell me he survived."

"He's fine," I say. "He's with me. He's with me all the time."

Halli closes her eyes and sighs. "Thank you." She reaches over and picks up my laptop from where it's sitting beside her on the curb. "I only ran inside for a second to get this. You have wi-fi out here. I know all about that now."

She hits Enter—no sweeping or poking, just plain old Enter—and the laptop finds a familiar contact.

And a familiar face comes up on the screen.

"She's here!" Halli tells him.

Professor Whitfield leans closer to his screen. As if that will help him see me any better.

"Audie?" he says, keeping his voice down. "Is it really you? Are you really alive?"

"I'm alive, Professor."

He shuts his eyes tightly and rests his forehead against his hand. He stays like that for a good long time before opening his eyes again.

"Audie, I'm so sorry," he says. "This is all my fault. I thought . . . I thought—"

"I'm fine," I tell him. "I saved Halli—that's what I wanted to do. She's alive and I'm alive. It worked. You didn't do anything wrong. Everything's fine. We just need to figure out how to reverse it."

"Take her inside," Professor Whitfield tells Halli. "We need to talk in private."

Halli scoops up the laptop and carries it—and me—back into my house. I'm not quite comfortable in my own body yet. Even though Halli is in here with me, it's not like we're banging up against each other in the same small space. We're here in my mind at the same time—and neither of us takes up any room at all.

But it's weird going from one body to another with just that underwater feeling in between. It's going to take me a minute to adjust. But I wish it wouldn't take any time at all.

Because this is me again—me. Me walking into my house. Me seeing that old, ratty furniture, the yellow kitchen table, the stupid pictures on the wall.

"Where's my mom?"

"At work," Halli says.

"Is it really Saturday here?" I ask.

"Yes," Halli says. "Why? What is it where you are? Where are you?"

"What's she saying?" Professor Whitfield asks. "What are you two talking about?"

And that's when I realize that one of us—Halli, I think—has been moving my lips and speaking her part of it out loud.

I see if I can do that myself. Instead of thinking my thoughts to Halli, I try making them come out through my mouth.

"Professor?"

"Yes?"

"This is Audie. Can you hear me?"

"Is that really Audie, Halli?"

"Yes," she answers him. It all sounds the same. He must feel like he's losing his mind.

We go into my bedroom. At least it used to look like my bedroom. Now I barely recognize it.

I'll admit I'm a slob. I have better things to do than organize or clean. So I've gotten used to a certain level of grunge.

But in her time alone here, Halli has completely transformed the place. There's nothing on the floor. There's nothing on my desk except a pad of paper and a coffee mug holding pens and pencils. All my books are neatly arranged on the shelves.

"Wait a minute," I say, lifting my hand to open my closet door.

I stand there in total shock. "Where . . . is everything?"

It's just like Halli's closet at her house: bare except for a few shirts, a few pairs of pants, and maybe one or two skirts. And just three pairs of shoes, neatly tucked toward the back.

"I saved everything," Halli says. "But I started going through it one day, trying to see what I could wear, and I just couldn't stop."

"No, it looks . . . great. I just can't . . . believe it."

I don't know if she can feel what's happening, but I'm fighting hard so she won't.

"Audie . . ."

"No, it's okay," I say, clearing my throat. "I was gone. This was your life. Of course you should do it how you want."

"Is everything all right?" Professor Whitfield asks.

From the way the laptop is aimed, I don't think he can see what we're talking about.

"Yeah," I say. "Sorry. I got distracted for a moment. It looks so great in here, Halli—really. It's like a new room."

"We can put it back," she whispers. Or maybe she doesn't whisper it—maybe she's just telling me that inside my head. I don't know anymore whether I'm hearing things with my ears or with my mind.

"It's okay." I brush my finger under my eye. It's a stupid thing to care about.

"How much time do we have?" the professor asks me.

The truth is, that hadn't occurred to me.

"I don't know," I say. "This is so different from before. I really have no idea."

"We shouldn't waste time," he says. "So please make yourself comfortable. And then tell us everything that's happened."

59

There are some parts I leave out. They're not relevant to the science, and I'm not sure Dr. Whitfield would even be interested in knowing about Jake and me, for instance, or about anything going on with Daniel.

I'm not even sure Halli should know yet. I'm thinking it might be better to wait until we're closer to her taking over her life again. Then I'll fill her in so she knows what she's walking into.

For all the weird science I know Professor Whitfield has been involved in over the years, the man can still be shocked. He spends a lot of our conversation stroking his beard, nodding, shaking his head, stroking his beard. He asks a lot of questions, and I actually have some answers for him, but not always.

"What happened on this side?" I finally get to ask. "What did you see?"

"You came back, just like before," the professor says. "Nothing strange. But then when you spoke it was clear it wasn't you."

"Probably because I grabbed him by the shirt and said, 'Where's Audie? What happened?'" Halli says.

"Yes, that had something to do with it," the professor says.

"So a week has passed here?" I ask. "Only a week?"

"Yes," Professor Whitfield says. "You were in my lab last Saturday night."

"How did I jump three days ahead?" I ask.

"Well, that's one of the issues," he says.

I make Halli tell me more of the details: like how she got home, whether she got here before my mother came back from her trip, how my mother reacted when she first met her.

"There are definitely times when I know she thinks I'm acting odd," Halli says. "Like when I've forgotten things I should know—"

"Like how to drive the car," Professor Whitfield says.

"That was a challenge," Halli agrees. "Not very smooth at first, but I've been practicing."

"But . . . what about school?" I ask. "And my job?"

Halli gives me a fake cough. "Sick all week. Your mother says it's not like me."

"No, I never miss school," I say. "Everyone must be confused."

"Your mom thinks you've been pushing yourself too hard with the Columbia application. She wants you to take a rest."

Amazing. I remember when trying to get into Columbia University was the most important thing in my life. I was obsessed with it. Now I can't even remember what that felt like.

"So . . . you two talk?" I ask Halli. "You and my mom?"

"As much as I can," she says.

I press a little spot on my chest. There's an ache there I haven't had time to notice in the past week. But now it's like Halli has watered it, and it's suddenly sprung back to life.

Halli notices it, too. "Sorry," she whispers inside my head.

"It's not your fault," I answer back.

I take a deep breath. "So where do we go from here?" I ask Professor Whitfield. "How do we undo it? How do Halli and I get our lives back?"

60

Professor Whitfield strokes his beard. He pauses to take a sip of the coffee he's been replenishing for the last hour and a half.

"Obviously I don't know for sure," he says. "This has never happened before, as far as I'm aware. There's nothing in the literature . . ."

He's stalling, and I know it. Of course he doesn't know for sure, and of course there's nothing written about it in any of the science literature—that's not what I'm asking.

"Professor?" Something in his expression is starting to worry me.

He coughs into his fist. It's almost as fake as the cough Halli gave me just a minute ago.

"He's not answering," I tell Halli.

"I can see that," she says.

"Here's my concern," he says. "In every previous instance, the two of you were able to communicate. Toward the end we never had any trouble with the two of you finding each other—in fact, Audie, you'd gotten much better at it in just that last hour or so before you disappeared. Remember?"

I do. Up until then I always had to wait for Halli to be ready for me. The two of us would have to concentrate at the same time, then we could link up.

But one of the experiments Professor Whitfield had me do on that last day was project my vision or my thoughts or whatever outward, and find Halli on my own. Like my own tracking system, locating her wherever she was, and sending myself there.

"Okay," I say. "So?"

"So my concern is that you lost that ability. Halli has been trying to contact you this entire time, and she couldn't even say whether you were alive. You just . . . disappeared."

I can see he's building up to something, but he won't get to it. My heart is speeding up, waiting for it to hit.

"Why do you think that is?" I ask. "Why did we lose each other?"

"Because I think the situation with Halli . . . played out," he says.

"Played out?" Halli repeats. "What do you mean?"

I watch his face. And somehow I know. I know exactly what he's trying to tell us.

"He means the situation with the avalanche," I say. My tongue feels slow. Either I'm holding it back, or Halli is. Neither of us wants me to say what I'm going to say.

Professor Whitfield nods. "Yes. That's what I'm saying."

And now I can feel Halli understanding it, too. Something just clicked in her brain.

"You mean . . . I died?" Halli says.

Professor Whitfield nods.

"Body A, or Body B—whichever," I say, impatient with myself, "is gone. Forever."

"Yes," the professor says.

The three of us sit here in silence. But both Halli's and my minds are spinning.

"That's why we lost contact," I say. "Because the thread was broken."

"I believe so," he answers. "Yes."

"Whatever connection Halli and I had disappeared once she died."

"But I'm not dead," Halli says. "You're alive and I'm alive."

"A *version* of you is alive," Professor Whitfield corrects her.

"I made a new Halli," I say, and as soon as it's out of

my mouth, I feel like I'm going to be sick. "Halli 2—is that right, Professor?"

"I believe you are a new entity. Yes."

"Oh my . . ." I cover my mouth with my hand. I don't want to say anything or think anything right now. I wish Halli didn't have to hear it.

"I believe you split off a new universe," Professor Whitfield says. "We knew it was possible—that theory has been out there a long time—but I believe what we're seeing here is living proof."

I get up from the bed. I have to move. I have to pace. I have to get out of my skin.

"So I didn't save Halli—not Halli 1," I say. "Instead I pushed her body into some new parallel universe, and started over."

"But started over three days ahead," Professor Whitfield says. "With a different history of what happened in those three days."

"Halli 1 died on the mountain," I say. "Halli 2 was never there that day. Somehow I made a new universe where she went down on Sunday with Daniel and Sarah and Martin."

"That's impossible," Halli says.

I laugh darkly. "None of this is impossible anymore."

Professor Whitfield fills in another piece. "I believe that's why you have this new kind of connection—sharing the same body, instead of traveling physically to where Halli is."

"Because that's how this new universe works," I say. "And that's why the old way wouldn't."

"This is all speculation," the professor warns me.

"It's more than I've had for the last week," I answer. "It's better than nothing."

Although it's actually worse than nothing, because before I had hope. And now I'm realizing—

"So we can never switch back," I say. It's just hit me like a blow to the back of my head. "That old Halli doesn't exist anymore. I'm not just holding her body for her, waiting for her to come back.

"No, I think you *are* her now," Professor Whitfield agrees.

"What do you mean, we can't switch back?" Halli asks. I can hear the stress in her voice. "I'm not you, Audie. I don't belong here."

"But you don't belong anywhere else, either," I say. "You're dead. In your other universe, you don't exist anymore."

"But I do exist," she says. "You're living in my body right now."

"No, that body was never you," I say. "It's only ever been me. This is a whole new universe—don't you understand? When it split off, the only Halli who lived was the one with me stuck inside. That's all that universe has ever known."

"So?" Halli says. "We can teach it something else. Put me back in there and put you back in this one."

"How?" I ask her. "That's the whole point—I don't think it can be done."

"That's what we're saying," the professor agrees.

"Listen, you two," Halli says, sitting my body up straight and tall. "We can't just give up. We're going to try—of course we're going to try. There has to be a way —you're just not thinking of it."

I hear a sound from the other room. The front door opening and closing.

"Audie?"

I freeze. "Mom?"

"I brought you some soup," she calls, but I don't wait to hear more. I'm on my feet in an instant, out my bedroom door, racing toward the living room, toward a long, necessary hug from the person I miss the most.

I'm halfway down the hall when I feel my body ripping apart.

61

I scream in a way I never scream, but it's not just the pain this time, it's also the loss. I was so close. I could have seen her. I never even saw her.

My skull feels like it's aflame. My head hurts so badly I wish I could just twist it off my neck and throw it away and beg for someone to bring me a new one. Every nerve of my body feels like there are little explosions still going on, and if I could just dip my whole self in ice maybe it would help.

"Jake!" I shout. "What are you doing?"

"What are you doing?" he says back. Daniel is holding on to me, trying to help me through it, and now I can see there's a little crowd gathered inside the door: Jake and Bryan and Sarah.

And Bryan is in the process of filming me.

"Get out!" I shout at him and the others. Then I press my hands against my head because shouting just made it worse.

"Sarah, take them out of here," Daniel orders her. "Leave us alone. Can't you see she's hurt?"

And those are exactly the words Jake doesn't need to hear.

He rushes to me now, tries to pull me away from Daniel.

"Halli! What's wrong? Tell me what's happening."

"Nothing is *wrong*," Daniel says, "except the three of you bursting in here. Get that camera away! Sarah, take them out!"

Sarah looks frightened and unnerved. There's too much shouting and chaos.

Meanwhile I can barely see, the pain is so bad. I'm bent over, trying to breathe through it, with both Daniel and Jake fighting to take care of me.

"She needs to go to a doctor!"

"What she needs is for you all to leave!"

And then suddenly it becomes a real fight. The two of them are pushing each other.

I back away because I don't want to be hurt anymore, and I'm bent over and paying attention to my shoes, and not them, but I hear the grunts and the blows, and the next thing I see is Daniel lying at my feet, the skin beneath his eye reddened, his bottom lip split and bleeding.

Then Jake rushes to me again. "We have to get you to a hospital. Sarah, call an ambulance."

"No!" I shout. "I'm not sick. Just leave—all of you leave."

"Sarah," Jake says, "GO."

She takes off at a run. I see Bryan in the corner, still filming us through his binoculars. I lurch my way over to him and do something that would make Olga proud. I slap my hand across his camera, smashing it to the ground.

"Get. OUT." I say. "Both of you. NOW." Then I hold my head again because it feels like it's going to explode.

Jake grabs my arm. And now he's pulling me out of the room.

Red runs along side me, pressing against my leg, the same way he did that very first day when I met him. He kept my bare legs warm. He was my friend. He's still my friend.

"Daniel?" I shout behind me.

He's already on his feet, coming to get me.

Jake lets go of me for a second, squares up, and hits Daniel once more, hard against the face. Daniel stumbles, goes down.

"Jake! Stop it!" I shout. And now I'm crying because everything I say is making me hurt so badly I want to vomit.

"You need help," he tells me. "You're hurt. I'm getting you to a doctor."

"I don't need a doctor," I mumble, before proving him right by passing out.

62

I am lying on my back.

Looking at a dark, unfamiliar sky.

And rolling somewhere fast, even though I can't move.

There are people all around me, shouting to me, shouting to each other, and I see lots of those binoculars around, all of them pointing toward me, but I don't care.

There's a dog running beside me, barking.

I try to move my arms, but I can't. I'm strapped down. I'm being pushed. I'm on a gurney, I think, because I'm covered in a blanket and strapped down, just like I've seen on TV shows.

"Miss Markham? What's happened?" a British man

calls out. Another one shouts, "Miss Markham! Did one of them hit you?"

I turn my head to see who asked me that, and catch a glimpse of why he even raised the question.

Daniel is under a street light, being attended to by someone in a blue uniform, and his face looks like he's just been in a boxing match. His eye is swollen, there's blood on his cheek, and his split lip is now at least double its normal size.

He brushes off the hand of whoever's working on him, and rushes over to me.

"What's happening?" I ask him.

"They're taking you to the hospital."

"I don't need a hospital—you know that."

"I'll come along after you," Daniel says. "Don't worry."

And now tears are seeping out of my eyes.

Red is barking and trying to jump up on the gurney with me. The person wheeling me keeps pushing him off.

"Somebody take this dog!" he shouts.

"No!" I cry. "He's mine!"

"I'll take him," Daniel says. "Halli, don't worry. We'll sort this whole thing out."

Now I'm being loaded into the ambulance. Red tries to hop up with me, but the blue-uniformed workers stop him. They're too rough—I hear Red yelp as he falls back the wrong way.

"Daniel?" I shout.

"I've got him," he says. "I'll take care of him. Everything's going to be all right."

Someone shuts the ambulance doors, and I can still hear the dog barking outside.

"Can't he come with me?" I try to sit up again, but a hand on my shoulder gently pushes me down.

"It's all right, Halli," Jake says. "I'm here with you now. You don't need Everett."

"I was talking about Red . . ." But I'm too tired. I give in to the tired and close my eyes.

The ambulance starts wailing out that horrible, awful song you hear in British movies—so much worse than American sirens, for some reason. It wails and whines and makes sure I know this is the absolute worst moment of my life.

Jake kneels to one side of me while a worker sits on my other side taking my pulse, checking my pupils, all of it.

Jake fishes for my hand under the blanket. He can't lift it out of there because it's strapped down too tightly.

"I love you, Halli," he says. "You'll be all right."

"No," I say, tears leaking again into my hair. "This is all wrong, Jake. You don't understand—"

"I love you," he says again. "I'll take care of you."

I close my eyes and try to block out the siren. Try to block out my head. Try to forget who I am. This isn't happening. Just a short time ago I was back in my house, back in my room, about to have soup with my very own mother. What happened to that girl? I want to be her. Can't I be her again?

Maybe I can. Maybe that's the answer.

I silently call to Halli.

I try to lift myself over the waves, find her, dive down.

But the siren screams and Jake talks lovingly to me, and there's too much noise all around me. Please, everyone shut up. Let me escape. Let me go find my life.

"You'll be all right," Jake keeps saying. "They're going to be able to help you."

No one can help me now.

I'm trapped and I can't get out.

SEIZE THE PARALLEL
CHAPTER 1

I can't blame Halli for what she did. She knew she was dead. I know now, too.

What do you do when your real life is over, and all you have left is this one? You do the best you can. And if you're Halli Markham, you do a better job than I've been doing, pretending to be her.

"I'm not like you," she told me. "I can't be you." I know that. Any more than I can be her.

But that's what we're doing, both of us. Living our opposite lives, messing them up in so many ways, maybe improving them in others.

So I don't blame her, for most of it.

Just for that one thing.

But that one thing—I'm not sure I can get over it.

When Halli was growing up, she and her grandmother, Ginny, did a lot of dangerous things: exploring the Amazon; climbing the Himalayas; rowing across the Atlantic; trekking to the North and South Poles. The list goes on from there—Ginny Markham was a world explorer, a world adventurer, and she took Halli everywhere with her from the time Halli was a baby.

But even though their adventures were dangerous, Ginny always emphasized two things: one, that preparation is the best defense against everything that can go wrong. And two, when everything goes wrong anyway, face up to it and keep on going from there.

So Halli learned to anticipate. And Halli learned to adapt. To look at her situation with a cold, hard eye, and not wish things were different than they were, but to deal with exactly what was happening at the moment.

So if a rope failed, a bone broke, if Halli and Ginny were lost somewhere in the middle of a violent storm, Halli learned to be quiet. To stop. To assess her condition, her surroundings, her options.

Is it any wonder, then, that once it sank in—the conclusion that Professor Whitfield and I had come to that the real Halli was dead, and I hadn't saved her from that avalanche at all, but instead had split off a new parallel universe where the only Halli who had ever existed was this new Halli 2, the one who was actually *me* inside Halli's body, and there would be no way to reverse it because the original Halli was gone, that connection severed forever—was it any wonder that a calm came over Halli, and she started thinking about what she had to do?

Especially once I disappeared again, ripped out of the body—my old body—that I'd been able to visit temporarily and share with Halli somehow. Now I was gone, and no matter what Halli and Professor Whitfield tried over the next several hours, they couldn't bring me back.

So as night fell, and my mother was calling to the daughter she thought was me, asking her what kind of takeout she wanted, and Professor Whitfield told Halli they'd have to try finding me again in the morning, Halli was already thinking about what to do next.

Because just like Ginny said, if things go wrong, you have to be able to rely on yourself. No point clinging to a rockface after your climbing partner has just fallen, and crying because it's all so sad and frightening. You'd better figure out a way to save yourself. You can cry about it later.

So Halli began making a plan.

Life in a parallel universe
takes everything you've got.
SEIZE THE PARALLEL
PARALLELOGRAM
BOOK 3

Read all four books in the series

PARALLELOGRAM SERIES
RobinBrande.com

Mena's first week of high school?

DISASTER

But things are about to evolve...

**Riley is an expert with dogs.
With people? Not at all.
But maybe her dogs can help her
finally find her own pack.**

SPECIAL CODE FOR PARALLELOGRAM READERS

Treat yourself to a soft, comfy, custom-made T-shirt designed by Robin Brande herself, inspired by the *Parallelogram* series and her other books! You can see all of them at robinbrande.com/collec tions/t-shirts.

And here's a secret just for you: Use the discount code **AUDIE10** at checkout to get **10% off any items in the store**. That means books, T-shirts, hoodies, mugs—whatever! Go ahead and treat yourself. And high-five, book lover.

Embrace your nerd

Sleep-Read-Repeat

About the Author

Award-winning author Robin Brande is a former trial attorney, black belt in martial arts, Reiki Master, and wilderness medic. She writes in multiple genres, including young adult, mystery, fantasy, and science fiction.

She is also a designer and maker whose work celebrates the bookish life.

You will find all of her many books and designs at:
RobinBrande.com